Thomas Hennessy

The Happy Hollisters
and the Indian Treasure

BY JERRY WEST

Illustrated by Helen S. Hamilton

GARDEN CITY, N.Y.

Doubleday & Company, Inc.

NOTE

The author acknowledges his indebtedness for much of the Indian information in this story to Popovi-Da, former Governor of the Pueblo of San Ildefonso, and to Gladys Blair Gilmour of Indian-Detours, Santa Fe, New Mexico.

Although the town of Agua Verde and the Yumatan tribe are fictional, the incidents are based on the lives and customs of the Indians in the Southwest.

Printed in the United States of America

Contents

CHAPTER 1

A Lost Puppy

PRETTY, ten-year-old Pam Hollister heard a clattering and banging which sounded as if it were coming from the front yard. Wondering if her younger brother was up to one of his tricks, she ran from the house onto the front porch.

"Who's making that dreadful noise?" she exclaimed. "Is it you, Ricky?"

At that moment a reddish-haired boy of seven, with freckles and mischievous eyes, raced into sight. "Did you call me, Pam?" he asked.

His sister, brown-eyed and golden-haired, smiled at Ricky. "I thought maybe—oh!" she exclaimed. "There's that noise again! What do you suppose it is?"

Ricky listened. The racket was somewhere down the street, so the two children hurried to the sidewalk to see what it was.

In the middle of the block, running toward them, was a little black cocker spaniel. A can was tied to the end of his tail. Frightened, the puppy was running faster and faster. Suddenly Pam was horrified at another sight.

"Look out!" she shrieked at the dog. A car was heading directly toward the little animal!

There was a screech of brakes and the driver stopped a few feet from him. Now the puppy was so terrified that he huddled at the curb shivering. Pam rushed up to him.

"You poor little creature," she said soothingly, stroking his head to calm him.

Ricky patted him too and untied the can from the puppy's tail.

"Who would play such a mean trick on a sweet little fellow like you?" Pam asked as she lifted him into her arms comfortingly.

The cocker had stopped shivering. He wagged his tail and licked her hand.

Ricky untied the can from the puppy's tail.

"We'll have to find out who owns you and take you home," she told him.

They walked back toward their rambling home on the shore of beautiful Pine Lake. As they reached it a boy and two girls ran to meet them.

"Did the car hit the puppy?" the boy asked.

He was twelve-year-old Pete Hollister, a sturdy lad with blond crew-cut hair and sparkling blue eyes.

"No, he wasn't hit," Pam answered, setting the spaniel on the ground.

"I'm glad," said the taller of the other two girls, starting to play with him. She was Holly Hollister.

She was six and looked a good deal like Ricky with her cute turned-up nose. Only Holly had brown eyes and dark hair, which she wore in pigtails.

"Can we keep him?" asked the little girl, Sue, the baby of the family. She was four and had deep dimples about which she was always being teased.

"I'd love to keep the puppy," Pam replied, "but I guess we'll have to find out where he lives."

"He'd be a wonderful playmate for Zip," remarked Holly, who did not want to give him up.

"Hey, where is Zip?" Ricky asked.

He gave a shrill whistle and the Hollisters' handsome collie came bounding from the back yard. He sniffed the puppy's face, then gave a happy bark.

"Zip likes him," said Sue. "We ought to keep the puppy."

"I'm sure his owner would miss him," Pam remarked. "It wouldn't be fair."

"See what we have, Mother."

Wondering if his name and license number might be on his collar, she leaned down and pushed his black, curly hair away from it.

"Here's the puppy's name and address," she said. On a little silver band was inscribed:

BLACKIE
Property of Indy Roades
62 Cedar Street

Ricky sighed. "Now we'll sure have to take him back."

"Let's show Blackie to Mother first," Holly suggested.

She carried the puppy into the living room where

an attractive, young-looking woman, with glossy blond hair was sewing.

"See what we have, Mother," Holly said, putting the puppy in her lap.

"Why, he's adorable," she remarked, stroking his ears. "Who owns him?"

"Someone named Indy Roades," Pam told her.

"That's an unusual name. I wonder if he could be the man who was a famous baseball player a few years ago."

"If he is, I want to be the one to take Blackie back," Pete spoke up, his eyes sparkling.

Mrs. Hollister suggested that he and Pam return the dog at once.

The other children went to the back yard to continue a game of store they had been playing. The Hollisters loved to pretend they were running their father's business—a combination hardware, sporting goods and toy store which he called *The Trading Post*. Sue stood behind the counter which was an orange crate.

"What can I sell you?" she asked Ricky. "A leaf tennis racket?"

"I'm sorry, Mrs. Storekeeper," her brother replied, "but I don't think so until you put some tape on that stem handle."

Ricky said that anyway he did not wish to play store any more.

"I want to go and find out what meanie tied the can to Blackie's tail," he told the others.

"I do, too," Holly said. "How will we do it?"

"I know!" Ricky replied. "We'll play a game. You walk down one side of the street and I'll go along the other. We'll ask everybody we meet if he saw anyone tying a can to a dog's tail."

"But we can't go off the sidewalk," Holly suggested. "That would spoil the game."

"No, and the one who steps on a crack first loses."

Holly dashed across the street and yelled, "One, two, three, go!"

The two children hurried along, running, skipping and side-stepping to avoid cracks. They asked several people they met about the tin can, but none of them had seen anybody bothering dogs in this fashion.

Presently Ricky met Dave Mead, a friend of Pete.

Holly nearly made it.

His answer was the same as the others, but he promised to try to find out.

Holly, meanwhile, had come to a fairly wide piece of sidewalk that had been freshly laid. Two masons were putting away their trowels when she raced up.

"Oh dear! I can't get past!" she moaned.

"Walk in the street," the older workman said grumpily.

"But I can't. It's against the rules of the game."

She ran back a few steps, then raced forward toward the fresh concrete. Reaching the edge of it, Holly made a flying leap over the new sidewalk.

But she did not quite make it, and landed up to her ankles in the oozy cement! Waving her arms wildly, she fell backward, sprawling full length in the middle of the gooey mass.

"Now look what you've done!" the older man cried out angrily. "We'll have to trowel that place all over again!"

"Oh, I'm so sorry," Holly said, tears glistening in her eyes. "I didn't mean to."

The younger mason was kinder. He took hold of the girl's hands and helped her get up.

"Accidents will happen," he said. "I have three little girls of my own, so I know."

By this time Ricky had come across the street and stood grinning at his sister. She was a pretty bedraggled sight. Wet cement was dripping from her clothes and from the ends of her pigtails.

Blackie rode in Pam's basket.

"We'd better go home right away," he said, and they hurried off.

Meanwhile, Pete and Pam had gone to Cedar Street on their bicycles, with Blackie riding in Pam's carrier basket. Number 62 was a ranch style brick house with a bright purple colored front door.

The door was opened by a short, stocky man of thirty-five. He had jet-black hair, high cheek bones and a reddish-tan complexion. The collar of his plaid shirt was open, showing a silver and turquoise necklace he was wearing. Pete and Pam decided he must be an Indian.

Upon seeing Blackie, the man grinned. "So you've been found, you rascal!" he said and took the dog in his arms. As he rumpled Blackie's fur, he said to the Hollisters:

"Thank you for being so kind. This scamp of a puppy disappeared yesterday—he was on the front lawn one minute and gone the next."

"I'm glad we found him for you," Pam said.

"Mr. Roades," Pete asked, "were you ever a baseball player?"

"I sure was," the man replied with a big smile. "That's when I got the nickname of Indy. And what are your names?"

When Pam told him his eyes widened.

"Oh, I've heard of you. People call your family the Happy Hollisters."

"Yes," Pam replied, smiling. "Mother, Dad and the five of us children have lots of fun together."

Then Pete said to the man, "You're an Indian, aren't you?"

"Yes, I am an Indian."

"Yes, I am. From the Yumatan Pueblo in the mountains near Agua Verde, New Mexico. You probably never heard of my tribe. It's a small one, with only a few families left."

Indy said that when he was a boy, the tribe had been driven from their reservation by a drought. Many of the Indians had left for distant places and never returned. But a handful, including several of Indy's family, had gone back about ten years before when the government had drilled a deep well, giving them a good water supply.

"But you didn't return with them?" Pete asked.

"No. By that time I was a big league ballplayer. But when I retired five years ago, I did go back to join my family. They were searching for a blue gem turquoise mine that once supplied the pueblo with a good income. It was buried many years ago in a landslide caused by terrific rains following the spring thaw of snow in the mountains.

"But my people still dream that it will be found," he sighed.

Indy told the Hollisters he had decided to leave the reservation and come to Shoreham to sell Indian-made articles. Many of these he received from the Yumatans. Pete and Pam said they hoped Indy's pueblo would find the turquoise mine.

"We must go now," Pam added.

Indy thanked them again for returning his dog and waved as the children pedaled off on their bicycles. All the way home they talked about the lost mine.

"Just think," said Pete, "a treasure buried in the mountains!" He turned into their street.

"And they can't find it," Pam sighed.

"Say, Pam, wouldn't it be great if—"

"Listen!" his sister interrupted, hearing the same kind of noise that she had noticed an hour before.

The children looked back. Zip was racing along behind them, a tin can tied to his tail!

CHAPTER 2

A Pillow Fight

HOPPING off their bicycles, Pete and Pam ran to where Zip was trying to shake the tin can from his tail. As Pete untied it, Pam bent down to hug her pet.

"It's a shame!" the girl said. "First Blackie and now you, Zip. I wish I knew who did it."

"I'll bet it was Joey Brill," Pete guessed. "Who else would be so cruel to animals!"

Joey was a boy Pete's age who also lived in Shoreham. He had played several mean tricks on the Hollister children.

Pete and Pam mounted their bicycles again with the dog bounding along behind them. As the riders turned into their driveway, Holly and Ricky ran up to meet them. Pam told them about the tin can.

"Dave Mead was here and gave us a clue," Ricky reported excitedly. "He saw Joey Brill tying a can to a dog's tail."

"So he is the meanie!" Pam exclaimed.

"Somebody should tie a can to Joey," Ricky said angrily. "Maybe that would teach him a lesson."

16

They got ready to play a trick on Joey.

Pete snapped his fingers. "A swell idea! Come on, Ricky! Let's do it."

Together the boys ran to the garage, where Pete had seen two empty coffee cans and a piece of old clothes line. He quickly punched a hole in each can and ran the rope through them.

"Are you really going to tie these on Joey?" Ricky asked, grinning in anticipation.

"Sure thing. I think we'll need Dave Mead to help us."

The brothers hurried down the street to Dave's house. They found him whittling a stick on the back porch. Dave clicked his knife shut and smiled when he heard the Hollisters' plan for playing a joke on Joey.

"I'm all for it!" he chuckled. "I saw him chasing a cat down by the lake a while ago."

The boys began their search. But when they heard a cat yowling behind a clump of trees near the lake, it did not take them long to locate Joey. Carefully concealing themselves, they watched as the bully tried to tie a rusty can to the protesting animal.

Pete stepped forward to confront the mean boy. Although Joey was only twelve, he was taller and heavier than most boys his age. He often used his size to advantage in making life miserable for smaller children in the neighborhood.

"Let that cat go!" Pete said firmly.

"Ha, ha! Says who!" Joey gloated.

Pete did not reply. Instead he gave the bully a hard shove, sending him head over heels and letting the cat free. As it raced up a tree, Joey sprang to his feet, fire in his eyes.

"I'll get you for this!" he shouted, lunging at Pete.

But Pete Hollister was ready for him. Stepping aside, he tripped Joey, who fell flat on his face. Immediately Pete gave a sharp whistle. Dave and Ricky rushed from their hiding places, and together the three boys held Joey down.

"Hey! Let me up! Get out of here! I'll call the police!" he shouted.

The boys paid no attention. While Pete and Dave held him down, Ricky stretched the rope across the mean boy's back and tied each end of it to the top of his arms. Then they let him up.

Joey tried desperately to shake the clanging tin cans off his back. When he could not do this, he wiggled and squirmed to loosen the knots. But Ricky and Dave had done a super job.

"You won't get away with this!" he shouted, running toward the street and making a fearful clackety bang noise.

By the time Joey reached the sidewalk, the clanking cans had attracted the attention of several other children.

"Ho, ho! Look who has cans tied to him!" they laughed. "Serves him right!"

As Joey ran on, even the grown-ups smiled. The boy grew more angry by the minute. The story spread quickly through Shoreham. When Mr. Hollister came home that evening, he said various customers

"These are very fine."

had laughingly talked about it at *The Trading Post*.

"We'll have to watch Joey," Pete remarked. "He probably will try to get square."

Pete told his father about Indy Roades and the puppy they had returned to him.

"Dad," said Pam, "couldn't you sell some of Indy's articles for him at *The Trading Post?*"

"That's not a bad idea," Mr. Hollister replied slowly. "I believe people who come to my store might be interested."

Mrs. Hollister thought so too, and it was decided that Pete and Pam should accompany their father to Indy's home after supper to talk to him about it. When they arrived, the Hollisters found the Indian playing with Blackie on the front lawn. Pam introduced her father, who explained what he had in mind.

"I'd like very much to have you sell my Indian articles in your store," Indy said, inviting them into the house to look at them.

What an attractive place it was! Besides some unusual looking chairs and tables the place was filled with Indian vases of many shapes and colors. Trinkets set with silver and turquoise lay about, together with brightly painted drums and small rugs of odd designs.

"These are very fine," Mr. Hollister said, examining them.

It ended up with his giving Indy a big order and both of them thanking the children for making the meeting possible.

"If you would like more Yumatan articles at a real

bargain," Indy said, "I know of a shop which is selling out."

"Where is it?"

"In the land of my people," Indy continued. "Old Juan Deer, proprietor of *The Chaparral*, is in poor health and must retire. You should go out there and look it over, Mr. Hollister."

Pam looked at him. "Perhaps the whole family could go," she broke in hopefully. "We'd learn a lot about Indians."

"And look for the Yumatans' lost mine," her brother exclaimed excitedly. "Have you any clues, Indy?"

"Only one," Indy answered. "I once met a circus rider who was a Yumatan. He said he had heard a legend that the lost mine was at Pilar Punta."

"What's that?" Pete asked.

"It's a high point of rock. I tried to locate it," Indy sighed. "But no luck. There are many pillars in my part of the country."

Mr. Hollister said he would think over the *Chaparral* proposition. If he wanted to buy its contents he would let Indy know. On the way home Pete asked:

"Dad, how about a trip out West to see Juan Deer's shop?"

His father smiled. "Well, I might do it when Tinker gets back. He's been ill, you know."

Tinker was a kind old man whom Mr. Hollister had engaged to work for him soon after they arrived in Shoreham. Tinker was a faithful employee but right now he had been out for a week.

"I know what!" Pam exclaimed. "Maybe Indy Roades could work at your store and help Tinker."

"Not a bad idea," her father replied.

He drove the station wagon into the driveway and the children hopped out. When they told their brother and sisters there was a chance they might go to New Mexico and hunt for a turquoise mine at Pilar Punta, Ricky let out a war whoop.

"Swell!" he cried and started to run around the dining room table. Then he knelt down and peered under it. "I'm looking for a turquoise mine!" he shouted. "Who wants to come with me?"

Holly and Sue joined in the game immediately

The boys were carrying on a red-hot fight.

and raced around the house, peeping into closets and cabinets. Mrs. Hollister, all smiles, watched them play awhile, then she reminded the younger ones it was past their bedtime.

While they were upstairs getting ready, Mr. Hollister sent a telegram to Juan Deer, asking the Indian for details about the articles he wished to sell.

Up in his room Ricky found it hard to settle down. Presently he stood on his bed and picked up a pillow. Suddenly he said to Pete:

"Look out for me! I'm a big Indian chief from Pillow Punta. And I'm on the warpath!"

With that he threw the pillow and hit Pete squarely on the head. Pete retaliated by grabbing his own pillow and in a few seconds the boys were carrying on a red-hot fight.

When Holly heard the noise, she poked her head into the boys' bedroom. Seeing the fun, she went for Pam and the two girls returned with their own pillows to join the battle. Wild whoops and yells filled the air.

Sue, hearing the noise, brought a small pillow from her bed and tossed it at Ricky.

"Goodness, what's going on?" thought Mrs. Hollister and raced up the stairs.

Just as she reached the doorway of the boys' room, Ricky picked up Sue's pillow and flung it with all his might. It hit the bed post with a bang, splitting open and sending a shower of feathers around the room.

"Now you've done it!" Pete shouted.

She locked the door on the outside.

"Stop, all of you!" Mrs. Hollister cried, and the children calmed down immediately. "Oh dear!" she said, looking at the split pillow. "I've had that since I was a little girl. I hope it isn't ruined!"

Ricky went over and put an arm about his mother. "I'm sorry, Mom," he said. "I'll fix it for you."

"All I ask is that you clean up this mess," she said. "Put the feathers in a pillow case. I'll do the rest."

Ricky obediently got a clean case and picked up the feathers, with the other children helping.

The following morning, Pam was the first one awake. Shaking Holly by the shoulders, she whispered:

"Let's make up to Mother for that pillow fight last night."

"Sure. How'll we do it?" Holly asked.

"By cooking Sunday breakfast for her as a surprise," Pam replied.

"Okay."

The girls hurriedly put on bathrobes and slippers and went to awaken their brothers. When they told the boys their plan, Pete and Ricky said they thought it a good idea.

The children dressed quickly and tiptoed downstairs one by one. As Holly, who was last, walked past her parents' room, she paused. Suppose Mother and Dad should come down before the surprise was ready!

"I'll fix that," she decided.

She quietly opened the door, removed the key and locked it on the outside. Then without making a sound, she scooted downstairs to the kitchen.

Fifteen minutes later Mr. and Mrs. Hollister awoke. The big house was strangely silent.

"I don't hear a sound," she said, glancing at the clock. "It's late for Ricky to be asleep."

Mr. Hollister said he would go and see if everything was all right. He strode across the room and grasped the door knob. It turned but the door did not open.

"Elaine," he said, "we've been locked in!"

CHAPTER 3

Dog Mischief

AFTER tugging once more on the bedroom door, Mr. Hollister decided to do something else. He suspected the children had locked it but what were they up to? He put on his trousers and shirt. Then he opened the screen of one window and stepped out onto the sloping roof over the porch.

Suddenly he smelled bacon frying. Grinning, he stuck his head back through the window and said to his wife:

"Don't be alarmed, dear. I have a very good idea of what's going on. I'll be right back."

Reaching the edge of the roof, Mr. Hollister dangled his legs over it and felt for the post. Then he shinnied down and landed unharmed on the ground.

Taking a front door key from his pocket, he let himself into the house and stepped as quietly as a cat to the closed kitchen door. He looked through the crack. The children were busy preparing breakfast. Their father turned, hurried upstairs and unlocked the bedroom door.

26

"Are the children all right?" Mrs. Hollister asked quickly.

"Happy as larks," he reported. "They're down in the kitchen making a surprise breakfast. Come on, we'll play a joke too!"

"How?"

"Disguise ourselves and walk in on them."

Mrs. Hollister chuckled and went for two old masquerade costumes from a hall closet. She put on a Spanish dress and dark glasses and covered her hair with a scarf. Her husband wore a black suit with a high hat and a mustache and beard.

"They'll never recognize us," Mr. Hollister laughed. "Come on! Follow me out the front door."

The two went around the house to the kitchen door and knocked. Holly opened it.

"Ahem, ahem!" the masquerading daddy began. "Do Meester and Meesis Holleestair reside here?"

"Yes, they do," replied Holly, staring at the strange looking couple. "But they are still in their room."

"Would you call them please? We must see them at once!"

The other children came to look at the callers as Holly disappeared upstairs. A moment later she came running back.

"They're not here!" she exclaimed.

"What!" said Pete. "Where did they go?"

"Oh goodness! I don't know. I locked them in!" Holly declared.

"You did, did you?" Mr. Hollister said in his natural voice and both parents whipped off their disguises.

The children's eyes opened wide. "Daddy! Mommy!" they shouted. "You fooled us!"

Then Holly added, "I didn't mean to scare you, locking you in. We just wanted to surprise you with breakfast to make up for the pillow fight."

"Well, you did," Mrs. Hollister said, smiling. "And everything smells so good. I'll get Sue. Then let's eat."

When they finished, Mr. Hollister declared he had never eaten a better meal. "How about surprising us every Sunday?" he said. "Only you won't have to lock us in. We'll wait to be called to breakfast."

After they had been to church and eaten dinner, the children sat down to look at story books, when the telephone rang. It was a telegraph message from

"Do Meester and Meesis Holleestair reside here?"

Juan Deer which Mr. Hollister jotted down and then read to his family. The Indian was asking a thousand dollars for the stock of *The Chaparral*.

"That sounds like a real bargain," Mr. Hollister remarked. "I think that when Tinker gets back to the store, I'll go out there and look it over. Maybe Indy will come and help Tinker."

"Let's ask him, please!" Pam urged.

This time the whole family went in the station wagon to meet the nice Yumatan. They found him clipping his front hedge. He put down the shears and walked over to the car. Mr. Hollister introduced his wife, Ricky, Holly and Sue, then said he had heard from Juan Deer.

"I'm going to wire him to hold the stock until I can get out there and look at it," Mr. Hollister explained. "Right now my head man is just recovering from an illness. Indy, would it be possible for you to work at *The Trading Post* while I take my family out to Yumatan country?"

"I'd like nothing better, Mr. Hollister," the ex-ballplayer replied with a grin. "When would you want me to start?"

"You'd better come tomorrow, so I can show you where things are."

"Thank you. I'll be there early," Indy said. "But I'll have to take Wednesday off. I promised to have a booth at the Grove County Fair with Indian things in it."

The nice Indian was clipping his hedge.

"You mean you're going to have a booth full of Indians?" Sue piped up.

Everyone laughed and Indy said, "No. Just all sorts of articles made by the Yumatans. Juan Deer wrote that he sent a large box of things to me. Only it'll be addressed to Edward Roades. That's my real name. I expect it to arrive tomorrow."

"What are they going to have at the fair?" Pete asked.

"All kinds of amusements," Indy answered. "Maybe you'd all like to come even though it is pretty far from here."

"Yikes!" Ricky shouted. "I want a ride on the ferris wheel."

"And I want a merry-go-round ride," Sue said.

Mrs. Hollister smiled and said she would drive the children over to the fair on Wednesday. In the mean-

30

time they would get ready to go to New Mexico and Indy would learn about *The Trading Post*.

By Tuesday noon the children's suitcases were partly packed and when their father came home to lunch they began asking if he had decided when they would leave.

"I'm waiting now to hear from the airline office," he said. "We'll fly most of the way."

"That's super!" Pete cried, his eyes shining with excitement.

"We've never been in a plane," Holly said. "Are we going to sleep in it?"

"Perhaps."

After that all the children seemed to be talking at once. Finally, when it was time for dessert, Mrs. Hollister asked Pam to go out to the back porch and bring in a lemon meringue pie she had left there to cool. Her daughter rose from the table and went out. But a moment later the others heard a startled cry.

"It's gone! Most of the pie's gone!"

Everyone rushed to the porch and gazed in dismay. Nothing was left but the crust!

"Oh dear!" Mrs. Hollister exclaimed. "Who did that?"

At first no one could even guess. Then Ricky said he had seen Zip sniffing near the table.

"My dog wouldn't have such bad manners as to steal pie," Pam said loyally.

"I'm afraid," Mr. Hollister answered, "that when

"Most of our pie's gone!"

it comes to food as delicious as Mother's pies, a dog would forget his manners."

"Let's find Zip," Ricky proposed.

The children saw the collie lying in the shade of a willow tree near the lake shore. He rose lazily to his feet and walked over to them.

"Did you eat our pie?" Holly asked him, shaking a finger at Zip.

"Oh, you did!" Pam cried out. "I can see some of it on the end of your nose."

Sure enough, on the tip of the dog's black nose was some meringue. As Zip hung his head, Pete could not help making a wisecrack.

"You're not a collie, Zip," he said. "You're just a little old lemon meringue hound!"

"You'll have to come in and 'pologize to Mother," Sue scolded the dog.

They led Zip into the house and told her he was guilty.

"Well," she said, "the only punishment I can think of for Zip is to make him eat the rest of the pie and not get any dog food."

"Wow!" Ricky burst out. "What a swell punishment!"

Mrs. Hollister gave each of the children an apple for dessert. As they were munching them, they heard the telephone ring. Pete answered.

"This is Indy Roades," the caller said. "Is your Dad there? I thought maybe he could help me out."

"He has gone back to the store," Pete replied. "Can we help you?"

"I guess not, thank you. That shipment from Juan Deer hasn't arrived. I just called the express company and the post office but it hasn't come to Shoreham. And tomorrow will be too late. I'm afraid it's lost."

"Golly, that's too bad, Indy," Pete replied. "I sure hope you find it."

After he hung up, Pete told Pam the bad news.

"I wish we could help Indy," Pam said.

They went outside and sat down on the front porch steps. Presently Mr. Barnes, the mailman, arrived. As he held out a children's magazine to them, Pam suddenly had an idea.

"Mr. Barnes," she asked, "how do you find packages that get lost in the mail?"

"There are several ways," he replied. "Sometimes a package goes to a wrong town because of a faulty address. Why, did you lose something?"

Pam told him briefly about Indy Roades and the missing package of Yumatan trinkets.

"Indy Roades, eh?" Mr. Barnes repeated the name slowly. He looked up at the sky thinking hard. Then he said, "There's a street called Indian Road in West Shore across the lake. Perhaps the package went to someone there by mistake."

"That's a neat clue!" Pete said. "I wish we could go over there and find out. Could you help us, Mr. Barnes?"

"Mr. Barnes, how do you find lost packages?"

The mailman said he would be glad to. "I'll tell you what," he said. "When I finish my deliveries at four o'clock, I'll drive back here in my own car and take you to West Shore."

"That's wonderful!" Pam said delightedly. "We'll tell Mother."

At ten minutes past four, she and Pete were waiting when Mr. Barnes drove up.

"Hop in," he smiled, opening the door.

Half an hour later they arrived in West Shore.

"I think Indian Road is up this way," he said, making a turn. "Yes, I see the signpost. And we're lucky," he chuckled. "There are only four houses on one side of the street and six on the other. It won't take us long to find out if any of these people received Indy's package."

They divided the work, each taking three, but met in front of the last house without any success.

Pam sighed and whispered to Pete, "Do you suppose our clue isn't any good after all?"

"We'll try this last house," Pete said, starting up the front walk.

Pam followed. When her brother rang the bell, a boy appeared and opened the screen door.

"Did you get a big box by mistake?" the girl asked.

"Why do you want to know?" the boy asked flippantly.

Pete and Pam had glanced inside the hall. Near the door stood a large carton. Pete read the sender's

"Did you get a big box by mistake?"

name printed in the upper left-hand corner. *The Chaparral!*

"I believe that's the package we're looking for," Pete declared, stepping forward.

"No, it isn't! It doesn't belong to you!" the boy shouted.

He slammed the screen door and locked it.

CHAPTER 4

An Indian's Secret

"MR. BARNES," come here!" Pete cried out. "Please!"

The mailman hurried up the walk to see what the trouble was. When the children told him, he rang the door bell.

Getting no response, he rapped loudly. Still no one came to answer it.

"I work for the United States Government!" Mr. Barnes called out. "You must answer!"

Soon they heard someone coming rapidly down the stairs. A woman opened the door and stepped onto the porch.

"What's wrong?" she asked.

Mr. Barnes explained and she apologized for her son's rudeness.

"A strange package did come here," she went on. "Please step inside."

Mr. Barnes and the Hollisters followed her into the hall and looked at the address on the box. It was crudely printed and read:

EDWARD INDIAN ROAD
WEST SHORE

"Edward is Indy Roades' first name," Mr. Barnes said.

"And Edwards is our name," the woman explained, "so that's how the mix-up occurred, I suppose. I was going to give the box back to our mailman tomorrow to return to *The Chaparral*. My son wanted to keep it, but of course I would not let him."

"Thank you for helping us," Pam smiled.

Mr. Barnes carried the carton of trinkets to the car and Pete and Pam suggested that they drive directly to Indy's house with it.

"Fine," the mailman said.

When they arrived, Mr. Barnes stayed in the car while Pete and Pam went in with the package. Indy was preparing a delicious smelling supper. Seeing the package, he smiled broadly.

"I can hardly believe my good fortune!" he exclaimed happily. "How'd you locate this?"

After Pam told him, Indy thanked the children.

"What is it you're cooking?" Pam asked, sniffing the wonderful aroma.

"It's a Mexican dish called posole," Indy said as he went into the kitchen to stir the food.

"Um. What's it made of?" the girl continued.

"Hominy, pieces of pork and chili," the man said, smiling. "It's very popular in the Southwest." He spooned a little into a small dish and offered it to the children. "Try it."

Pete and Pam tasted the unusual food and both said they liked it.

"When you go to Pueblo Land," Indy said, walking outside with his callers, "you will find plenty of Mexican and Spanish dishes. Many of the people there are descendants of the Spanish, who came to that part of the country four hundred years ago."

"That's interesting," Pam said. "Some day will you tell us more?"

"Tomorrow," Indy promised. "I'll tell you about my niece and nephew too."

Pete and Pam said good-by, expecting to see their friend the next afternoon. However, early the next morning he stopped at their house and said he wanted them to help him arrange his booth at the County Fair.

"I'll ask Mother," Pam said.

She gave her permission, saying she would bring

Indy pried open the top of the package.

the others later, and the children hurried to Indy's car. By the time they arrived at the fair an hour later, the place was bustling with activity. Men were putting up tents. Carpenters were finishing booths and women were covering them with bunting and colorful crepe paper.

Indy parked, then swung the large box from *The Chaparral* onto his left shoulder and walked toward a small booth. Reaching it he set the package down and pried open the top. As he lifted out some of the articles, Pam exclaimed in delight and Pete said:

"Oh boy, these are swell!"

There were fancy blankets, lovely Indian dolls, beaded moccasins, pretty red and blue drums, pottery, beadwork, silver and turquoise jewelry.

"I've never seen lovelier things in my life," Pam remarked. "It looks like—like Christmas!"

"Let's arrange small pieces first," Indy suggested. "Then I'll take out the larger ones."

Pete and Pam worked with him to arrange the articles to best advantage on the three tiers of shelves. Then the Indian unpacked more objects.

"Bows and arrows!" Pete exclaimed, picking up an Indian archery set. "May I try this, Indy?" he asked, twanging the bowstring.

The Yumatan said that he would be glad to let Pete use it a little later. "But right now," he continued, "will you children decorate the booth for me while I go to the official tent to register? The hammer and tacks and fancy paper are in the car, Pete."

Pete spoke to the Indian cowboy.

"We'll do it," Pam answered.

Her brother got them and they started tacking up the bright-colored decorations. As they were finishing, Pete and Pam heard the clatter of horses' hoofs. Turning, they saw a line of cowboys coming along single file on Pinto ponies.

"I didn't know they were going to have a rodeo," Pete exclaimed. "This is keen!"

After the riders had passed by, another group of men trudged behind them leading several fierce-looking longhorn bulls and a few Brahman cattle.

"Crickets!" Pete yelled. "Do you suppose they're going to ride them? I'll ask one of the men."

He ran over and spoke to the last cowboy in line. He was a little older than the others and was dressed in a bright velvet shirt, blue jeans and brown deerskin moccasins. His long black hair hung in two braids on either side of his weatherbeaten face. Around his neck he wore wampum and silver beads.

When Pete asked the Indian whether any of the men would try to ride the bulls, he replied: "Yes. Cowboy stay on bull very good."

At that moment he spied Indy's booth. He shuffled over to it with a queer expression on his face.

"Yumatan!" he said, picking up a piece of pottery with a cloud and arrow design.

"Yes, they are," Pam replied. "How could you tell?"

"Yumatan cross arrows like this," he said, pointing.

"Do you know the Yumatans?" Pete asked him.

The Indian replied that he was a member of a tribe which lived close by the Yumatans. Then he said, "Me War Horse. Like Yumatan. Good Indians. Work hard. Make nice things."

Suddenly his eyes lighted on a silver snake ring. War Horse reached forward to touch it and smiled.

"You buy silver snake ring?" he asked. "Owner have good luck."

He hurried off to catch up with the rodeo cowboys.

"Good luck?" Pam asked, raising her eyebrows and staring at the ring. "Maybe we *should* buy it."

When Indy returned a little later, they told him what had happened.

"I thought a snake was bad luck," Pete said.

"Oh, no," Indy replied, a smile spreading over his broad face. "Snakes are little brothers to the Indians. They carry messages to the spirits deep in the earth. That is why some Indians dance with live snakes when they pray for rain."

"I'd like a good luck ring," Pam remarked. "If I wear it, perhaps we'll find the lost mine."

"Take it as a present for helping me," Indy said, handing the shiny ring to Pam.

"Oh, thank you!" she exclaimed.

"You're very welcome. You are good children, just like my niece and nephew." Before Pam had a chance to ask about them, Indy continued. "By the way, your mother has arrived with your brother and sisters. They'll meet you at the ferris wheel."

"Let's go, Pam!" Pete cried.

They raced toward the giant ferris wheel which loomed high into the sky on the far side of the fair grounds. They found the other Hollisters and Pete bought tickets.

"Let's ride in cars on opposite sides of the wheel,"

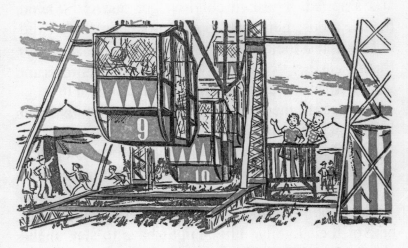

Then the wheel went around.

he proposed. "Then we can wave to one another."

"All right," his mother agreed and told the man to arrange it this way.

"Okay," he grinned. "You're the only passengers, so you can make the rules."

Mrs. Hollister stepped into one of the double cars with Sue, Ricky and Holly. Then the wheel went around. When they were at the top, it stopped and Pete and Pam got into the car at the bottom. After they were seated, the ferris wheel started again. Round and round it went.

Each time Pete and Pam were opposite the others, they would all shout and wave.

"Toot toot!" Ricky imitated a train. "See you next week!"

A few moments later, when Pete and Pam were on the ground level, the ferris wheel gave a sudden jolt and stopped. The two children got out and waited for the amusement ride to start up again. But it did not start and the owner came out excitedly, saying to them:

"First time I ever had trouble like this. The cog-wheels are jammed and the machine won't move until I get a new part for it."

"You mean my mother and my brother and sisters can't get down?" Pam exclaimed in alarm.

"That's right. Maybe not until tomorrow."

The Hollister children stared up at the other members of their family. They might have to stay in the air all night!

"But we just have to get them down!" Pam cried.

Pete thought quickly. "Maybe the firemen can rescue them."

"Now that's an idea," said the man. "Suppose you go call them, son."

As Pete ran off to a telephone, the ferris wheel owner cupped his hands and called to Mrs. Hollister, "Don't get nervous! We're bringin' the fire department to get you!"

"Yikes!" said Ricky.

He was the first one to spy a red hook and ladder as it turned off the highway and drove across the fair grounds. While its siren wailed and a big red light blinked off and on, people hurried from all directions.

"We're going to be saved!" Holly cried.

"We'll go down a ladder just like from a burning building," Ricky shouted.

Sue was rather frightened and clung tightly to Mrs. Hollister. As the hook and ladder came to the base of the ferris wheel, the crowd cheered. The firemen slowly raised a ladder. Up, up, up it came, until it reached the side of the car.

A fireman, moving with the speed of a monkey, raced up the ladder. But as he neared the top, it began to dip away from the car.

"This will never work," the fireman called out. "The car isn't steady enough to support the ladder. We'll have to try another way to rescue you."

"How?" Mrs. Hollister asked, concerned.

"Do you think all of you could jump down into our big net?" the fireman asked.

"Oh!" Holly cried.

Ricky's heart pounded like mad.

The fireman hurried down the ladder, and it was drawn back onto the truck. Then he and the other men took out a large life net and opened it. Standing in a circle, they held on to it tightly beneath the car in which the Hollisters waited.

"Jump!" one of the men called.

"I want to go first!" Ricky cried, pulling himself to the railing of the car.

The net looked much smaller than it was.

CHAPTER 5

Bows and Arrows

FROM the Hollisters' high perch at the top of the ferris wheel, the net below them looked much smaller than it actually was. The fire captain shouted up again:

"Jump!"

"Here I go!" Ricky yelled.

Mrs. Hollister put an arm around his shoulder and kissed him. "Be very careful and jump straight," she warned.

Ricky took a deep breath and stepped off into space. Down, down he went, the wind whistling past his ears. Then with a soft thud, he hit the net. After bouncing a few feet into the air, he settled into the net and scrambled to the edge.

"Ricky, that was wonderful!" Pam cried, hugging him.

As the onlookers shouted and clapped, Pete said with a grin, "It was just like in the circus."

Ricky stuck out his chest. "I think I'll be a high wire man someday."

Holly had been watching carefully. When she saw that her brother had landed safely, she stood up ready

47

Holly hurtled downward.

to go next. With her pigtails flying, she hurtled downward and landed in the net. Again cheers arose from the crowd, as Holly was lifted out.

"You children have no fear at all!" a woman praised them as Pam hugged her sister.

"I—I was a little scared," Holly admitted, as she looked up at her mother and Sue.

Mrs. Hollister was holding the little girl in her arms. A second later she came whizzing down and landed squarely in the middle of the net. They gave two bounces and then were helped to the ground by a friendly fireman.

As the applause died down, several people shook hands with Mrs. Hollister, praising her family's bravery and saying how glad they were it had not been necessary for her children to stay in the ferris wheel all night. She smiled a little breathlessly, brushed her hair back in place, and thanked them. Then she added laughingly:

"I think my three younger children have had enough excitement for one day—and me too. We'd better go home." She turned to Pete and Pam. "You may stay and help Indy, if you like. Dad will come later and pick you up."

The children decided to remain at the fair. After the others had left, they made their way back to Indy's booth. A few customers were there, examining the unusual trinkets and Indy had already made several profitable sales.

When he saw the children, he smiled. "I'm glad you came back," he said. "Business is good and I need your help."

Pete and Pam stepped behind the counter. As the lovely Indian articles were purchased, they wrapped them.

During a lull half an hour later they were surprised to see their father walking toward them.

"Dad, how did you get here?" Pam asked, knowing that Mrs. Hollister could not have reached home to give him the station wagon.

Her father explained that the store had a large order of nails to deliver to a carpenter who was building a house not far from the fair grounds.

"So I brought them over in the truck," Mr. Hollister said.

"Dad, you should have been here to see the excitement," Pete said and told of the ferris wheel incident.

When he finished Mr. Hollister laughed. "Whew! What a family of daredevils I have!" Then he added, "You children must be hungry. I'll take you to lunch. How about joining us, Indy?"

The Yumatan said he was hungry too and would like to join them. He packed the articles that were left and locked them up. Mr. Hollister found a pleasant outdoor restaurant at the edge of the fair grounds, where they ordered soup and sandwiches.

When they finished and were on the way back to the booth, Pete stopped them at an archery range.

"Wait! Let's see how an Indian can shoot," the boy said.

At first the athlete was reluctant to try his skill.

Indy took aim.

"When I was a boy I could shoot pretty straight," he said. "But I haven't done this in many years."

"Oh please," Pam urged.

Indy stepped into the booth. Picking up a bow and an arrow, he took aim, then let go. The arrow whizzed into the center of the target.

"Crickets!" Pete shouted. "You haven't forgotten a thing about shooting!"

The Yumatan smiled and shot another arrow into the golden center of the target, then he scored two more very close to it.

"Now you try your luck, Pete," Indy suggested, paying the attendant.

The boy's first arrow fell short, the next went over the target.

"Wow!" Pete exclaimed. "I really need some practice."

He fitted another arrow into the bowstring. As it landed far back of the target, he saw a boy sneak out from behind some bushes to grab the fallen arrow.

"Joey Brill!" Pete cried out. "He would do something like that!"

The attendant ordered Joey off the archery range. Scowling, the boy walked back a distance but stood watching as Pete prepared to shoot again.

"Aw, you're no good!" Joey shouted. "You couldn't hit the side of a barn ten feet away!"

The taunt made Pete nervous. He laid down his bow and took a deep breath. Then picking it up again, he took aim once more and twanged the bow.

51

The arrow zinged past him.

Joey, thinking Pete had given up, dashed out to grab more arrows from the grass just as Pete shot. Pam screamed and Mr. Hollister yelled:

"Look out! Duck!"

Pete was paralyzed with fright as the arrow sped directly over the target toward Joey's back. Then he gulped in relief as Joey fell flat on the ground and the arrow zinged above him.

"That crazy boy!" the attendant shouted, running toward him.

But Joey, scared, scrambled to his feet and raced off into the crowd. The man turned back, saying:

"Well, I'm glad we're rid of him."

He offered Pete a few more shots, but the boy decided he had had enough. The scare had left him a bit unnerved.

As they left the booth, Pam thought of something to take his mind off Joey. She whispered to her father and when he nodded, she turned to her brother.

"The rodeo is going to start in a little while," she said. "Why don't you go with Dad and watch it? I'll help Indy."

Pete grinned. "That would be swell."

"You go too, Pam," Indy insisted. "I can take care of the booth alone. Most of the pieces have been sold already."

"All right."

The children said good-by and set off with their father. The rodeo was being held in a field at the edge of the fair grounds. On one side was a barn with a fenced-in yard and several large pens. Around the other three sides were wooden bleachers.

Mr. Hollister bought tickets and the three went in. Presently several steers were released. Then with whoops and shouts the cowboys rode out, lassoing them and doing all sorts of rope tricks.

Finally, it was time for the Brahman bull riding contest. The gate to one of the pens was raised and out lunged a huge black bull, with a cowboy astride his back. The bull stopped short, throwing the rider over his head.

As the man rose to his feet, another bull with a rider charged into the center of the ring, bucking and jumping up stiff legged. In a moment the fellow on his back went flying into the dust.

"This is terrific!" Pete exclaimed. "Those cowboys didn't last long. Say, look over there on the rail of that pen! An Indian is trying to get on the next bull."

"It's War Horse!" Pam cried.

The bull stomped so furiously that War Horse could not mount him. The Indian decided to try calming the animal. Climbing down the rails, he walked into the ring and pulled something from his pocket.

"It's a snake!" Pam exclaimed, as the Indian brandished the reptile in front of the bull.

"He said our silver snake ring was good luck," Pete ventured. "Maybe he's trying to charm the bull."

As he quickly told his father about the strange Indian, War Horse put the snake back into his pocket and climbed the rails of the pen. The bull had quieted down so the Indian was able to jump on his back.

"The snake did bring good luck," Pam giggled. "But who'd want a live snake in his pocket?"

"Not a girl," Pete grinned.

The gate was raised and in a flash the bull dashed to the center of the ring. He wheeled, tossed and lowered his head, and kicked up his hind legs. But War Horse hung on grimly. The Indian held his right hand high in the air, as the bull violently tried to unseat him.

"He'll win the prize!" Pete shouted. "He's staying on longer than any of the others!"

Just then a bell rang. The contest was over. The Indian had won it!

"Look what he's doing now," Pam said, as War

War Horse hung on grimly.

Horse leaped off the animal and drew the snake from his pocket.

The Indian began to walk up and down in front of the audience, dangling the reptile and grinning. As he neared the section where the Hollisters were sitting, he suddenly tossed the snake toward the crowd. Several women and girls shrieked and Pete shouted:

"Look out, Pam, it's going to land in your lap!"

CHAPTER 6

A Farewell Party

WITH a little scream Pam tried to dodge the flying snake. But it hit her chest and tumbled toward her feet.

Both Mr. Hollister and Pete dived for the reptile. The boy's hand reached it first. Grasping the snake behind the head, Pete held it high in the air so it would not strike at anybody. To everyone's amazement the snake remained perfectly still.

"Maybe it's dead," Pam said, recovering from her fright.

As she said this, War Horse ran up. "Snake been dead a long time," he said, chuckling. "This only snake skin filled with wool. War Horse play joke."

"And a good joke," Pete grinned. "But we didn't get it."

When War Horse realized that no one had caught on to his trick, he apologized for scaring them and put the snake back in his pocket. Pam smiled at him.

"The snake was good luck for you, wasn't it? You stayed on the bull."

"Serpent always friend of Indian," War Horse replied.

He put the snake back in his pocket.

"Do Indians also have bad luck signs?" Pam asked.

This question changed the smile of the rodeo rider to a frown. "Indians not like to talk about bad luck," he said, shaking his head. "Like to be happy."

Pete, Pam and their father looked at one another. Apparently they had hurt the Indian's feelings.

"I'm sorry, War Horse," Pam said kindly. "We don't know your customs."

This remark seemed to make War Horse feel better for he turned around and smiled. "You nice children. I tell you story about Yumatan bad luck. They probably hear owl."

The children looked puzzled. "Owl?" they asked.

"Owl hoot. Bring Indian bad luck," War Horse said. "Indian no like to hear owl."

Then, as the Hollisters listened eagerly, he told them how a small branch of the Yumatan tribe, called the Turquoise Clan, had been digging gems in their mine at Pilar Punta many years before. Suddenly an owl had hooted and the next moment a landslide had buried the mine and all the people inside it.

"Didn't any of them get out alive?" Pete asked.

"No."

"That was terrible," Pam sympathized.

War Horse nodded. "Owl bad bird. Always unlucky to Indians."

"Do you know where the turquoise mine was located?" Pete asked excitedly.

War Horse thought for a moment before he replied. "Old Indian tell War Horse Pilar Punta in straight line toward rising sun from twin cave."

"What does that mean?" Pete questioned.

"War Horse not know. Nobody know. Many caves and canyons in Pueblo Land. All look alike."

At this moment the Indian was called to the judges' stand to receive his prize for the bull riding contest. As the Hollisters left the field, Pam said excitedly:

"That was a wonderful clue to the mine, wasn't it? If we can find the twin caves and walk directly east, we might find the lost turquoise mine."

"But first we'll have to find the twin caves," her father laughed.

When they arrived home the other children and Mrs. Hollister listened eagerly to this latest bit of news about the land of the Yumatans.

"Let's fly out there right away and find the brother and sister caves," Sue proposed.

The others laughed and Pam teased her, "Maybe they're twin girls or twin boys."

"No," said Sue firmly, "they're a boy cave and a girl cave." The little girl looked off into space. "One's a little higher than the other and fatter. That's the boy."

Sue's family always enjoyed her imagination and now coaxed her to tell them more about the caves. She was just in the middle of a story about how two pieces of turquoise came to life and rolled all the way to Hollister house to see her when the telephone rang.

Pete answered it and called his father. "It's the airline office," he said.

"It's the airline office!"

The whole family stopped talking and waited for his report about reservations to New Mexico. He was gone only a minute and came back smiling.

"We leave at two o'clock Friday," he said.

The children shouted in glee and the girls hugged their father.

"That's sure super, Dad," Pete said and Ricky picked up a pillow and threw it into the air.

When the excitement died down a bit Ricky and Holly decided to play an airplane game. They ran upstairs to get two model jets. Racing to the back yard, they wound them and let the toys go. The planes zoomed over the lake and back again.

"Mine's going to stay up longest!" Ricky cried gleefully, as Holly's plane started to come down.

But just then Ricky's nosedived after his sister's.

"Oh!" she cried. "They've hit!"

The planes locked and fell to the ground.

"My plane's ruined!" Holly exclaimed. "Why did you have to bump into me?"

"It wasn't my fault," Ricky said. "And look at my plane. One wing's broken off!"

"Well, let's mend them," Holly sighed, and they spent the next hour before supper gluing the toys.

During this time Pam helped her mother and talked over what they might do with their pets while the family was away.

"Maybe Jeff and Ann Hunter would take care of Zip and White Nose and her kittens," Pam said.

"Suppose you ask them," Mrs. Hollister suggested. "I'll leave it to you."

Pam telephoned her playmates, who lived down the street, and Jeff and Ann said they would be happy to take care of the Hollister pets.

"Instead of moving them, though," Ann suggested, "suppose we come to your house in the morning, at noon, and in the evening and feed them and let them out for some exercise."

"That would be fine. Thank you very much!" Pam said.

"Come tomorrow. I will show you where their food is."

At the supper table Mr. Hollister told his family more about the trip.

"We'll arrive late Friday evening a couple of hundred miles from the Yumatan Pueblo and stay at a motel," he said. "I've telegraphed that I'd like to rent a car and drive the rest of the way."

"Did you tell them a big one?" Sue asked. "There are lots of Happy Hollisters."

"Yes I did," her father smiled.

The next morning more suitcases were brought from the attic and the packing continued. In the midst of it Jeff and Ann came in. Jeff, who was eight years old, was a smiling boy with dark hair and blue eyes. His sister was ten. She had gray eyes, dark hair which hung in ringlets, and cute dimples. After Pam showed them where the cans of food and boxes of biscuits were for the Hollister pets, Ann said: "We want you all to come to a going-away party at our house tomorrow."

"Oh thank you," Pam said. "We'll be there. What time?"

"Eleven o'clock," Jeff answered. "It's for lunch just before you leave on your trip."

"Oh, that's sweet of you," said Pam.

The next day the five Hollister children, dressed in their traveling clothes, walked over to the Hunters. How lovely their yard looked! Two picnic tables had been placed end to end beneath a big apple tree. The table was covered with a gay cloth on which stood big platters of tasty-looking sandwiches and dishes of candy and peanuts. Ricky wanted to nibble on the nuts right away, but Pam warned him that he must wait until the Hunters started to eat.

The picnic was ready.

Other guests began to arrive. Twelve-year-old Dave Mead came first, holding something behind his back. He hid it under one of the benches before coming over to greet the other children. Dave was a good-natured boy and Pete's best friend. He had straight hair, and one lock always seemed to slip down over his left eye.

Donna Martin was the next one to skip into the yard. She was Holly's special playmate and was seven years old. Donna had brown eyes and she wore her brown hair in braids.

Mrs. Hunter glanced at her wristwatch and said, "We have one more guest still to come." And to herself she added, "I do hope he behaves himself."

She had hardly finished saying this, when Joey Brill leaped through a small hedge and dashed into the yard.

"He insisted upon coming," Ann whispered to Pam, then aloud she said, smiling, "Before we start the party, we want to give you Hollisters some presents."

Like magic, the other guests produced gifts they had brought. Sue received hers first; a small locket from Donna Martin, with a place for two pictures.

"If you see some nice Indians, you can put their pictures in here," Donna explained.

"Oh thank you," said Sue.

Ricky's gifts were from Jeff Hunter. There were two of them; one a ball and the other a big red balloon with Indians on horseback painted on it.

63

"This is swell!" Ricky exclaimed.

Dave Mead handed Pete a combination compass and jackknife. Holly was very pleased to get a pair of tiny binoculars from Ann. She could use them to look out the window of the airplane.

Now only Pam was without a gift. All eyes turned to Joey Brill. Did he have one for her? Instead of handing over a package Joey walked up to Pam his hands behind his back.

"Here's a real surprise for you," he grinned, extending his arm and popping something into the pocket of her dress.

The next moment the girl shrieked. Her "present" was wriggling around in her pocket.

"Joey!" she cried. "What—what is it?"

Pam looked down. Over the edge of her pocket

"You can have it back," Pam said.

peeped a tiny white mouse, his pink nose quivering. "Oh my goodness!" she cried.

"It won't hurt you," Joey grinned. "It's tame."

Pam scooped up the mouse in her hands. "Just the same, you can have it back," she said.

After the party the Hollister children hurried home. Indy was waiting to take the family to the airport and urged that they hurry. There was not a minute to lose, he said.

Everyone who had been at the Hunters' came to see the Hollisters off. They watched as one suitcase after another was piled into the station wagon.

Suddenly a mischievous gleam came into Joey Brill's eyes. Grabbing one of the smaller bags, he ran down the street with it.

"Stop that! It's mine!" cried Holly, racing after Joey.

Pete, too, took off after Joey. Halfway down the block, the mean boy realized that the others would certainly catch him. With a toss he threw the suitcase into the street. The bump broke it open and all of Holly's clothes spilled on the pavement.

"Oh, they're ruined!" Holly cried out. "Pete, help me pick them up."

"We'll miss our plane!" her brother said, worried.

CHAPTER 7

Fun in the Sky

"WE MUSTN'T miss the plane!" Holly said anxiously.

She and Pete quickly picked up the scattered clothes and flung them into the suitcase. By this time the other Hollisters had driven down the street. The two children hopped aboard with Pete holding the bulging, unfastened bag under his arm.

As the car started off, Mrs. Hollister took Holly's clothes from the bag and folded them neatly, while Pam arranged them in the suitcase.

"That Joey! What'll he think of next!" Holly sighed. "I'm glad we're going away."

"Indy," said Sue seriously, "we're going to do everything the Indians do!"

The Yumatan grinned and said he hoped she would have a fine time and learn a little Indian dance.

"And don't forget to practice with a bow and arrow, Pete," he said. "I know the Indian boys will be glad to give you some pointers."

As they drove toward the airport, Indy put one hand into his pocket and pulled out a letter. Handing it to Mr. Hollister, he said:

"This is an introduction to my uncle Swift Eagle,

the governor of the Yumatans," he said. "My uncle will be glad to show you around the pueblo."

"And how about your niece and nephew?" Pam asked him.

"Yes, please tell us. Who are they?" Holly begged, unable to restrain her curiosity. "I want to know some Indian children."

"You shall," Indy continued. "I have written to Red Feather and Blue Feather that you're coming."

"Oh goody!" Holly was bubbling over. "I can hardly wait to see them!"

Indy explained that they were grandchildren of Swift Eagle as well as being his niece and nephew. Red Feather was a ten-year-old boy and Blue Feather, his sister, was nine.

"They are orphans," Indy went on, "and live with Swift Eagle. Their parents died last year in a flash flood."

"That's too bad!" Pam said. "I feel sorry for orphans. I wish we could do something for Red Feather and Blue Feather."

"You will," Indy said, half smiling, "if you find the lost turquoise mine. Then all the Yumatans can have many things they can't afford now."

"Oh boy," declared Ricky enthusiastically. "We can go on an expedition and hunt for it."

Indy immediately was smothered with questions by the Hollisters. Could the Indian children speak English? Would Indy teach them a few Yumatan words before they reached the airport?

The children ran ahead.

"I think it would be fine for you to learn a few Indian words," Indy agreed. "What would you like to know?"

"How to say Red Feather and Blue Feather," Pete said.

"Red Feather is Tse-way-n-peh, and Blue Feather Tse-way-n-tsuwa."

After the Hollisters had repeated the words several times, Pam asked, "How do you say Indian boy and Indian girl?"

"A-nun-ka and ah-yu-ka," Indy replied.

By this time both Mr. and Mrs. Hollister had become interested in hearing about the language of the Yumatans, which Indy said was called Tewa.

"How do you say, 'How are you'?" Mrs. Hollister wanted to know.

Indy smiled. "On-segee-an."

"And 'good-by'?"

"Segee-de-ho," Indy told her.

Holly was so excited that she clapped her hands and exclaimed, "This is fun. We can talk Indian already. When I see Blue Feather I'll say, 'On-segee-an Tse-way-n-tsuwa'."

"Good!" Indy praised her. "In no time at all you'll be talking like a real Yumatan!"

By this time the airport had come into sight and Indy pulled up in front of the administration building. While Mr. Hollister went for the plane tickets inside the building, the Yumatan helped the boys with the baggage. Then he wished them luck and said good-by.

A porter came to take their luggage on a truck and Mr. Hollister had it weighed. Then he and his family went out through a gate, where a big plane was waiting.

The children ran ahead, climbed up the steps of the landing platform and walked in the door. There they were met by a blond-haired young woman in the trim blue uniform of a stewardess.

"I can see this is going to be a jolly trip with you children along," she smiled, taking Sue by the hand. "Take seats anywhere you please."

Since they had never been in an airplane, the brothers and sisters looked about them in awe.

"I didn't know a plane was so big inside!" Ricky exclaimed as he and Pete walked along the aisle toward the front.

On either side of the aisle were rows of two adjoining seats. The boys slid into seats on the left side, while Pam and Holly sat opposite them. Mrs. Hollister made herself comfortable behind the girls, with Sue next to her near the window. Mr. Hollister sat behind the boys.

A door at the front of the plane opened and another stewardess appeared. Through the doorway the boys caught a glimpse of two pilots seated before a large instrument panel.

"May we go in there?" Pete asked the stewardess.

"I'm afraid not," she replied, smiling. "It's a safety rule that no passengers may be allowed forward. But we can have lots of fun anyway once we're in the air."

As she left them, the giant engines roared to life one by one. Then suddenly a sign flashed on over the door in the front of the cabin:

Fasten Seat Belts.

As Mr. and Mrs. Hollister showed the children how to fasten the two ends of the straps across their laps, the plane started to move over the long runway.

"Hurrah! We're going!" Ricky shouted.

He pressed his nose to the window glass while the plane taxied to the far end of the airport. It swung around and stopped.

"Why aren't we going, Pete?" he asked in dismay.

"Our pilot's waiting for a go-ahead signal from the control tower," his brother replied.

All at once the airplane's engines began a throaty

roar again and the ship raced along the runway, then took off.

"We're in the air!" Holly cried gleefully. "On our way to see the Indians!"

The children looked down at the ground, which seemed to fall away from them as the giant plane climbed into the sky.

"There's the lake, and I can see our house!" Pam said excitedly.

The others looked too. Sure enough, there was the Hollister home on Pine Lake! It looked like a toy house, which grew smaller and smaller until it was out of sight.

By this time the plane was flying high over a beautiful, fluffy cloud bank. A pleasant voice came over a loudspeaker.

"We're in the air!"

"Welcome aboard flight 224. This is Miss Traver, one of your hostesses, wishing you a pleasant trip. Miss Gilpin and I will do all we can to make you comfortable. If you want anything, please push the seat button. Thank you."

At once Holly pushed the button. When Miss Traver came, the little girl said:

"Do I have to stay tied in all the time?"

The stewardess laughed and said no, only for the take-off and landing. She helped Holly unbuckle the belt, then the pretty, blond-haired stewardess walked to Mrs. Hollister's seat and said:

"I think it's wonderful to see a whole family traveling together."

"We're going to visit the Indians," Sue said. "Are you going with us?"

"Well, part of the way." The stewardess patted Sue's curls. "And if any of you children should become hungry, let me know."

"I'm hungry right now," Holly said, popping her head over the top of the seat.

"Me too," Ricky chimed in.

"We'll take care of that in a jiffy," Miss Traver promised and disappeared down the aisle into a tiny kitchenette. She returned with a platter of cookies and apples.

"Don't you have a banana?" Sue asked. She liked these better than apples.

"I'm sorry, no," the stewardess replied.

"Will you please go downstairs and get me

The boys carried on an imaginary attack.

one?" she asked, forgetting she was in the sky.

"Yikes!" Ricky laughed. "It's a couple of miles downstairs!"

"Indeed it is," Miss Traver said. "And any minute we may be higher."

Later, when Pete was looking out his window, he spotted another plane flying far beneath them. He pointed it out to Ricky.

"An enemy! Um-pow! Um-pow!" Ricky cried.

The boys continued to carry on an imaginary attack until the enemy disappeared into the clouds.

"I think we got him," Ricky told his brother.

After several hours had gone by, he began to hunt for something else exciting to do. Pete was working out a cross-word puzzle and the girls were busy looking at magazines which they had taken from a rack.

All at once Ricky glanced up and saw a tube over his head. He turned it, and a rush of air blew in his face. He pressed his seat button. This time Miss Gilpin appeared at his side.

"What's that?" Ricky asked, pointing to the tube.

"A ventilator," the stewardess replied. "The more you turn it the more air it lets in."

"Thank you," Ricky said, and turned it on all the way.

What a nice hissing noise it made! Holly stopped her reading and asked Pete to change seats with her. He moved across the aisle. After she and Ricky had played with the ventilator a few minutes, the boy said:

"Maybe it'll blow up the balloon Jeff gave me."

Reaching into his pocket, he pulled it out and attached the end of the tube. The balloon grew bigger and bigger.

"Stop!" Holly warned him. "You'll break it!"

The boy pulled the balloon from the ventilator, and let the air out with a funny squeaking noise. Several passengers started to chuckle.

"Let me blow it up this time," Holly begged.

Her brother let her do this, and when the toy was fully inflated, Holly released the air.

Zizz, zizz, plop!

The balloon whizzed from her hand and zigzagged through the cabin, finally hitting Mr. Hollister on the nose.

74

"Nice aiming, Holly!" Ricky said admiringly as everyone roared with laughter.

After his father handed the balloon back, the boy attached it to the vent again. It grew larger and larger.

"Look out!" Pam cried and Sue put her hands over her ears.

"It's going to burst!" Holly giggled close to Ricky.

All at once Holly's giggling was interrupted by a loud *BANG*. *The balloon burst right in her face!*

"Ow!" she cried, and she felt her head to see if everything was still there. But she was not hurt, only frightened.

Ricky meanwhile looked very sober, for the plane had started to nose down.

"Did I break the plane, too?" he asked Miss Traver.

"It's going to burst!"

CHAPTER 8

Stewardess Pam

MISS TRAVER smiled at Ricky's fear that he had damaged the airliner.

"No," she said, smiling. "We're going down because we'll land at that airport you see ahead."

"To get my banana?" Sue asked impishly.

The stewardess laughed and said the little girl would have to wait and see. They would be picking up their supper.

"Watch for a little cart," she advised. "It contains the hot food we're going to eat after we take off again."

Again the seat belt sign flashed and the plane banked toward the runway. After making a smooth landing, it taxied to the main building. The Hollister children eagerly looked for the cart. Pam was the first to spy a little truck speeding toward them. Painted on the side was:

J. B. Smith
Caterer

The driver stopped the truck alongside the landing platform and carried several metal containers onto the plane. While he was doing this a motor driven fuel wagon pulled up and filled the planes' tanks. Then two more passengers got aboard and soon the airliner roared off into the sky again.

As soon as Pam had unfastened her seat belt, she walked back to talk to the stewardesses. A minute later her family was startled to hear her voice over the loudspeaker:

"This is Pam Hollister speaking for Stewardesses Traver and Gilpin. We welcome you to flight 224 and hope you will be comfortable. Dinner will be served shortly. If there is anything special you wish, please press your seat buzzer."

"Hurray for Pam!" Sue said in a loud whisper to her brothers. "She's a good play stewardess."

The older girl came back to her seat a moment later, smiling broadly. "They said I could help out while they were preparing the trays," she said.

In a few minutes Miss Traver walked down the aisle, carrying a tray which she put in Pam's lap. Then she and Miss Gilpin served all the other passengers one by one.

On the trays were hot meat and vegetables and for dessert there was gelatin, but Sue got a special surprise. In the middle of her plate Miss Traver had placed a fat yellow banana!

"Goody!" she exclaimed. "You got it when we went downstairs."

After supper the hostesses tilted the children's chairs back and they napped while the sky grew

"We're getting off here."

darker. Four hours later the plane banked as the pilot prepared to land again.

"We're getting off here," Mr. Hollister said as he roused his sleepy-eyed children.

After they had said good-by to Miss Gilpin and Miss Traver, the children walked out. Mr. Hollister called a cab and they were driven to a nearby motel for the night.

After breakfast next morning Pete asked about the car in which they would continue their journey. At this moment a tall sunburned young man in tight-fitting blue jeans entered the motel and asked for Mr. Hollister. He was directed to their apartment and said he had a car for him to rent.

"We couldn't find a seven-passenger car for you,

Mr. Hollister," the man said, "so we're renting you an air-conditioned school bus. We don't use it in the summer."

"A school bus!" the children chorused.

The young man pointed to the parking area where the bus stood under a tree.

"Yikes!" Ricky clicked his heels and the children ran pell-mell toward the bus.

"This is a yummy game," Sue giggled, as she hopped in and flopped onto one of the leather seats.

Mrs. Hollister stepped aboard next, with the children following her.

"Dad, you're the bus driver!" Pete exclaimed. "And here's a cap you can wear."

He reached behind a sunshield and pulled out a khaki-colored cap which he gave to his father.

Holly giggled when he put it on. "Let's each give Daddy a penny for our fare," she suggested.

Each child did this. Then a porter came with their baggage on a hand truck. When it was stowed in the back of the bus, Mr. Hollister announced:

"All aboard! Away we go to Yumatan Land!"

He drove from the motel along a broad highway that stretched like a ribbon across the sandy desert country. Mr. Hollister asked his family to close all the windows and then he turned on the air-conditioner. In a few moments the bus became comfortably cool.

"This is very pleasant," Mrs. Hollister commented, looking out the window at the countryside.

Giant saguaro cactus plants grew alongside the road holding up their arms as if greeting the visitors. Pam said she had learned something about cactus plants in school.

"I think that big one up ahead," she said, pointing, "is a barrel cactus and there's water in the thick stems. It's said Indians used to drink it when they were lost on the desert."

After driving all forenoon, Mr. Hollister stopped at a roadside stand for refreshment and then started off again.

How different the country began to look after that! From the flat, arid desert they climbed into a range of hills. The vegetation became greener as they went higher and soon they came to a cool climate in the pine-covered hills.

"There's a big sign up ahead," Pete remarked presently. "I wonder what it says."

They climbed into a range of hills.

Mr. Hollister stepped on the brake so they could read it. The sign stated that the area ahead was a national park and that visitors were welcome. There was an inn for guests.

"And dancing bears!" Pam cried as she finished reading the sign.

"Oh, please let's stay over night," Holly begged. "I've never seen bears dance."

Mr. Hollister looked at his road map, then agreed. "We never could make the Yumatan Pueblo today. We may as well stay here."

The road gradually wound up a long hill. At the top was the inn. It was built in Spanish adobe style and sprawled over a half-acre of ground. Beautiful pine trees bordered the hotel and to one side was an immense cage with several brown bears in it.

"Oh, let's make them dance!" Sue begged.

While Mr. Hollister went to ask about rooms, the children ran to the cage. A guard standing there smiled.

"You've just come?" he asked.

"Yes," Pete answered. "When do you have the show?"

"Any time," the man answered. "I'll give you one now."

He opened a large wooden box nailed to a tree. Inside was a record machine, which began to play. In a moment one of the bears reared up on its hind legs and turned round and round.

"Oh, aren't they funny?"

"That's Sally," the man said. "Now watch Billy and Tilly."

Two bears stood up facing each other and put their front paws on each other's shoulders. Then they lifted each hind leg in turn, keeping time to the music.

"Oh, aren't they funny?" Pam laughed.

Ricky and Holly began to jump around imitating the bears. When the music stopped and the animals did somersaults, the children fell to the ground and flopped over too.

Mrs. Hollister called them to come, so they hurried to the inn. How attractive the Spanish and wild life decorations were! Ricky was particularly interested in a large mountain lion rug in the lobby. As he was stroking its head, Mr. Hollister said:

"Did you hear about the entertainment surprise for children tonight?"

"No. What is it?"

"Story-telling by an old cowpoke named Cactus Charlie."

"It sounds swell," Ricky said.

After supper all the children at the inn seated themselves cross-legged on the floor of the lounge before a roaring blaze in the fireplace. As Pete chatted with a boy named Jack he noticed that Ricky had not yet arrived. But he forgot about this when Cactus Charlie appeared.

From his ten-gallon hat to his silver spurs, Cactus was Pete's idea of a genuine cowboy. He swaggered before the fireplace as the children clapped, and said:

"Hi pardners! Would you like to hear about the time I chased Big Chief Bull Horn or about when I captured the giant mountain lion single-handed?"

"The mountain lion!" the children shouted.

"Okay!"

Cactus pulled a three-legged stool from beside the fireplace and sat down on it. As the children listened intently, he told of a giant beast that had frightened a herd of cattle and made off with several calves.

"The puma—that's the same critter—left tracks the size of saddle bags," Cactus drawled, "and might still be roamin' the range today if I hadn't stalked and battled the brute single-handed."

The cowboy told his wide-eyed listeners how he

had trailed the mountain lion and cornered him in a cave.

"I looked him straight in the eyes," Cactus said.

Suddenly Holly screamed and pointed to something moving in the flickering shadows. A huge puma head appeared and a deep growl filled the lounge.

The boys shouted and the girls cried out in fright. Even Cactus's eyes popped, and he fell off the stool. As the hotel manager came running, the mountain lion stood up straight and Ricky's face popped out from beneath the skin.

"Ha, ha! Fooled you, didn't I?" he chuckled.

The children laughed and Cactus admitted it was the best trick that had ever been played on him.

"You sure scared me," he grinned.

"Ha, ha! Fooled you, didn't I?"

Ricky put the skin back where he had found it and the story telling continued until bedtime.

Next morning Pam asked her mother's permission to take a short walk before starting their ride to the Yumatan pueblo.

"I want to look around and then feed the dancing bears," she said.

Mrs. Hollister said all the children but Sue might go. Pam stopped to buy a bag of popcorn, then the four children set off through the woods of pine and aspen trees toward a canyon a girl had told Pam about. Reaching it, they gazed in delight. How lovely the colors looked with the sun shining on the tops of a distant mesa!

After looking at the view a while they turned back. The boys ran on ahead and soon were out of sight. Pam and Holly strolled along slowly.

Hearing a sound behind them, they turned. Not far from them was a big bear! The girls were so frightened they could not move.

"Oh, Pam, what'll we do?" Holly whispered to her sister. "Let's run!"

Suddenly the animal reared up on his hind feet and walked quickly toward them!

CHAPTER 9

Swift Eagle

ALTHOUGH frightened, Pam Hollister knew she must think fast. What should she do about the bear that was coming toward her and Holly? They could climb a tree of course, but the girls remembered that bears can climb them too.

"Oh Pam, he looks so hungry!" Holly whispered.

This gave Pam an idea. Maybe the bear was not unfriendly after all—just hungry. He had probably smelled the bag of popcorn she was carrying and wanted it.

Pam gave the bag a great heave. It landed directly in front of him and opened. The bear stopped, sniffed and reached a paw inside. He put some of the popcorn into his mouth. Then apparently liking it he took the whole bag between his front paws and sat down on the ground to enjoy it.

Seeing this the two girls raced away. Both were out of breath by the time they reached their brothers. After they told them what had happened, Ricky wanted to go back and look at the bear. But just then their mother appeared and forbade this. They hurried on and Holly reported the exciting adventure to her

He sat down to enjoy it.

father and a bellhop who were packing luggage in the bus.

"That was quick thinking, Pam," Mr. Hollister said, putting an arm around his daughter.

The bellhop said that the bear was really tame, but that he had frightened several people recently with his appetite.

"His sweet tooth gets him into trouble," the man chuckled.

The Hollisters said good-by and stepped into the bus. Soon it was winding down the mountainside.

"Let's play a game," Sue suggested as they drove along.

"How about that song game, Dad?" Pam asked.

Once before on a trip Mr. Hollister had introduced this game to his children. He would whistle a few bars from the middle section of a tune and they had to guess what the songs were.

"Come on, Daddy, start," Holly said eagerly.

Her father smiled and began to hum part of a familiar song.

"Oh, I know what that is," Ricky said. "*Home on the Range.*"

"Right! One point for you!" his father replied.

In turn Mr. Hollister hummed or whistled sections from *Yankee Doodle*, *Dixie* and *The Star-Spangled Banner*. Sue, Holly and Pam each guessed a name correctly.

"Guess I'm the dumb one," laughed Pete. "Whistle another tune, Dad. I want to get a point."

Mr. Hollister was about to, when he suddenly jammed on the brakes. Everybody pitched forward as the bus came to an abrupt stop, its tires squealing.

"Did we hit something?" Sue cried out.

A quick glance out the side windows provided the answer. A coyote had run into the path of the bus, and only Mr. Hollister's quick action had spared the animal its life. The coyote scooted behind some tumbleweed and disappeared.

"Oh, I'm glad that baby dog didn't get hurt," Sue said. "I wish we could catch it."

"Mother wouldn't like it," her father said. "The coyote is really a wolf and destroys sheep and cattle."

When the bus started up again, the children played other games. Pete and Pam had a struggle naming all of the forty-eight states. Then Holly beat Ricky in a

88

spelling bee when her brother missed on *scissors*. But Ricky won the next game of naming the most makes of automobiles.

A few miles farther on, Pete spotted a mud spattered pickup truck parked at the right side of the road some distance ahead. They could not see whether anyone was in it or not.

"I wonder if the driver ran out of gas," Pam remarked.

As Mr. Hollister drove up and slowed down, an Indian stepped from the truck and flagged them to stop. The tall, handsome redskin had graying black hair, high cheekbones, and a friendly smile. He was dressed in khaki trousers and a brown shirt open at the neck.

Before he had a chance to speak, Holly climbed

An Indian flagged them to stop.

from the bus and asked with a smile, "Are you a Yumatan Indian?"

When he answered yes, she said, "On segee an?"

A look of complete amazement came over the Indian's face. He started to speak rapidly in Tewa. Holly shook her head that she did not understand.

Pam had stepped out of the bus and said to the Indian. "We know only a few words in your language, like Tse-way-n-peh and Tse-way-n-tsuwa."

The Yumatan looked more bewildered than ever. "Those are my grandchildren!" he exclaimed.

"Then you're Swift Eagle, governor of the Yumatans!" Pam burst out.

By this time all the Hollisters were crowding around him.

"This is very strange," said Mrs. Hollister. "We have a letter of introduction to you from your nephew Indy Roades."

"It's a tiny world even way out here," Sue sighed and the Indian laughed.

Mr. Hollister introduced his family, then Swift Eagle read Indy's letter.

"I haven't seen him in a long while," the governor said, leaning against his truck. "I'm glad to hear he's well."

"How are Red and Blue Feather?" Ricky spoke up.

"Fine. They'll be delighted to meet you," their grandfather assured the Hollisters. "I'll be happy to show you around the pueblo, if I can ever get back there myself."

"How would you boys like to ride with me?"

"Are you in trouble, Swift Eagle?" Mr. Hollister asked.

"Something's wrong with my engine," came the reply. "I wish I were a mechanic as well as a governor."

"Let me look at it," Mr. Hollister offered.

He examined the motor but could not find what was wrong with it.

"Suppose we push your truck to the next garage," he suggested.

Swift Eagle readily agreed. As he slid into the driver's seat, the Indian called to Ricky and Pete:

"How would you boys like to ride with me? I can tell you some stories about the Yumatans."

"Oh thanks, we'd like that," Pete answered.

The brothers hopped in quickly. When Pete signaled to his father that they were ready, the bus began to push the truck slowly along the road.

As soon as everything was going well, Pete told Swift Eagle about the rodeo he and Pam had been to, and how War Horse had given them a clue to the lost turquoise mine.

"Do you know where the twin caves are?" the boy asked.

"No, and I've never heard that twin caves would lead to the mine," he said.

He added that many years before, he had heard someone mention two old caves on the mountainside.

"Perhaps those are the twin caves you mean," he said. "I'll have to try to find them."

"If you do," Pete went on, "then War Horse said to walk east from there and you'll come to the mine."

Swift Eagle smiled. "I hope it will be as easy as that," he said. "Don't forget the mine is buried under tons of dirt from the landslide."

"But maybe the entrance isn't buried so deeply," Pete said hopefully.

Shortly before noon they came into a little town made up of a few small buildings. One was a post office, another a restaurant, and a third was a garage. Mr. Hollister pushed Swift Eagle's truck in front of the repair shop. Then they all got out.

"In return for your great favor," Swift Eagle said to Mr. and Mrs. Hollister, "I'd like your family to be my guests at lunch."

92

"That's very kind. We'll accept," Mrs. Hollister said.

While they were eating, Swift Eagle said he was sure the children would have a fine time in Agua Verde and at the pueblo.

"I'll tell my grandchildren you Anglos are coming," he said.

"What do you mean by Anglos?" Pam asked him.

Swift Eagle grinned. "I can see you are truly from the East," he said. "You will want to learn the expressions we use in the Southwest."

He went on to explain that the people who are not Indians or of Spanish descent are called Anglos.

"You mean I've been an Anglo all this time and didn't know it?" Pete grinned.

They all had a gay time at the luncheon table. By

They all had a gay time at the luncheon table.

the time they finished eating, Swift Eagle's truck was ready. He climbed into it and waved to the Hollisters.

"See you at Agua Verde. Let me know when you arrive!"

"Segee-de-ho!" the children called as they drove away.

"He'll get there much sooner than we will," Mr. Hollister told his family. "I find this school bus was not built for speed."

"Won't we get there today?" Holly asked.

"I'm afraid not," her father replied. "I wouldn't want to arrive after dark. We'll stop late this afternoon at a place I've read about. It's run by Mexicans."

When they drove up to it about six o'clock, the children said it looked just like pictures in their books. It was a low orange-colored adobe building with an open air garden in the center. This was filled with desert plants and flowers. Chairs decorated with gay designs stood among them.

As soon as Mr. Hollister had made arrangements for rooms, they walked into the attractive patio and sat down at a table. The proprietor, Mr. Ortega, dressed in a colorful Spanish costume, said that this hotel specialized in chili con carne. Would they like to try it?

Mrs. Hollister was not sure the children would care for it and ordered small portions for them to try.

"Chili con carne is made of beans and meat," she said, "and is seasoned with Chili pepper."

When the waiter brought their plates, Sue was the

first to put a spoonful into her mouth. What a dreadful face she made! After gulping it quickly, she reached for her glass of water, then exclaimed:

"This is made of fire! But—I guess—it's good!"

The others tasted theirs warily, but after a couple of spoonfuls they liked chili con carne. They also enjoyed eating sopaipillas, hollow bread which tasted much like doughnuts. The meal ended with Spanish melon and Holly declared she felt stuffed.

"Let's play hide and seek," she said.

Holly closed her eyes and began to count while her sisters and brothers ran to find hiding places. Ricky went so fast he suddenly tripped and reeled toward a spiny cactus. The boy tried to stop but lost his balance and sat down hard on the spiked plant.

"Ouch!" he shrieked. "The cactus bit me!"

"Ouch! The cactus bit me!"

CHAPTER 10

On Your Mark!

"HELP! Help!" Ricky yelled in pain as he tried to rise from the cactus plant on which he was sitting.

Pete and Pam rushed over to him. Each took one of their brother's outstretched hands and pulled him to his feet.

"Yikes! I hurt! I'm full of thorns!" he cried, dancing around.

By this time Mr. and Mrs. Hollister had heard their son's cries and came running to his side. Back of them was Mr. Ortega who had also heard the commotion.

Learning what had happened, he said the boy had been "bitten" indeed. The cane cactus he had fallen on was called a "biting cactus." He took Ricky by the hand and led him into the hotel office. Smiling at the others, who had followed him, he said:

"We'll be out in a minute," and closed the door behind them.

As the Hollisters waited, they heard Ricky give several squeals of pain and guessed that Mr. Ortega was pulling the prickly needles out of him. In a few minutes the door opened, and the boy walked out. He proudly told how Mr. Ortega had put adhesive

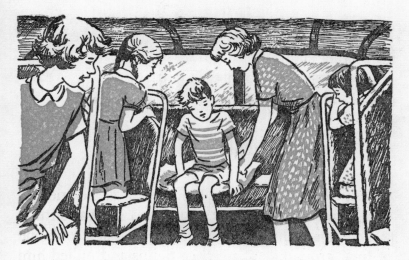

Ricky sat down gingerly.

tape over the thorns and then had pulled it off. Out had come the stickers!

"I guess now I'm Cactus Ricky," he said, managing a little grin. He found it impossible to sit comfortably and soon went to bed.

After breakfast next morning everybody was in his place in the bus with the exception of Mrs. Hollister and Cactus Ricky. Holly beeped the horn a couple of times to let them know that they were ready to go.

"Maybe Ricky's not well," Pam said, worried.

She was about to go into the hotel and find out when her mother and brother appeared. Mrs. Hollister was carrying a plump pillow in one hand. Without a word she put it on the back seat and Ricky sat down gingerly upon it.

"Now my cactus bites don't hurt," the boy said and his mother smiled.

In less than two hours the Hollisters came to a road sign reading:

AGUA VERDE   1 mile
YUMATAN PUEBLO   3 miles

"Hurray! Hurray! We're nearly there!" Holly shouted.

Presently they saw the first low, Spanish-type houses of Agua Verde.

"What are they made of?" Pam asked.

"Adobe bricks," her mother replied. "They're of sun baked mud."

"Yikes, I wouldn't want to live in one," Ricky said. "The rain might wash my house away."

"These bricks become very hard," his father explained, "and many mud houses have been standing hundreds of years."

Near the end of the main street stood a two-story adobe hotel which was deep pink in color. Several Indians were seated in front of it, colorful blankets wrapped around them. When Mr. Hollister stopped the bus, they got up and pulled trinkets from their pockets to sell.

Mr. Hollister shook his head, saying he expected to stay several days and would buy souvenirs later. He went into the hotel and inquired about rooms.

"We can give you three nice ones facing the mountain," the Spanish American clerk said.

Two olive-skinned young men carried the Hollisters' baggage inside. As they went up in the self-service elevator, one of the bellhops asked what had happened to the other Anglo children. The Hollisters looked puzzled.

"I mean the other children from your school."

"Oh," said Pam, laughing, and told him the Hollisters had rented the bus.

"I see," the bellhop said. "We often have bus loads of children coming here sightseeing. In fact, people come here in all sorts of vehicles and often they sleep in them."

The young men had just gone downstairs when there was a tap on Pam's door. She opened it to find two Indian children, a boy and a girl standing there.

"We're Red Feather and Blue Feather."

"We're Red and Blue Feather," the girl said. "I'm Blue. Grandfather sent us over from our pueblo to meet you."

"Oh hello," said Pam. "You're awfully nice to come. I'll call my family."

How attractive the Indian children were, Pam thought as she introduced the others. All the Hollisters liked them at once. Red Feather said he and his sister would like to show the Hollister children around Agua Verde.

"Will you let them come out?" Blue Feather asked their parents.

"That's very nice," said Mrs. Hollister. "But be back by lunch time."

The little group hurried off. Upon reaching the center of town, the Indians paused and the young visitors stared in admiration.

"It's all full of rainbow colors," Sue marveled.

There was a mixture of gold, red, brown, blue and white in the sidewalk shops that lined the public square. Indian women, seated on the ground, were selling colorful pottery and necklaces made of beads.

"You buy pretty things?" one after another asked hopefully.

"No," Blue Feather answered for the Hollisters. But to one pretty young woman she said, "Show us your water jug, please."

From beneath a beautiful red and gray blanket the woman took a small rust-colored vase with two spouts on it.

"This wedding cup," she said. "Husband drink from one side. Wife drink from other side."

"How interesting!" Pam exclaimed.

Then suddenly an idea came to the girl. Her mother and father would be celebrating their wedding anniversary soon. Maybe they would enjoy the jug as a gift from their children!

"Is this for sale?" Pam asked, and explained what she had in mind.

The woman looked at Blue Feather who said something to her in Tewa. Then the Indian handed the drinking vase to Pam, a broad smile on her face.

"I give this to you," she said. "You good friend of governor. I friend to you."

Pam was embarrassed but Blue Feather urged her to take it, saying she would hurt the woman's feelings if she refused the present. So Pam thanked her and put the vase under her arm.

"We'd better go now," said Blue Feather, "so we can see the races."

"They're for children," Red Feather added. "Would you like to go in them?"

"Yes," Pete answered. "You're certain it's okay?"

"Sure."

They walked over to the side of the plaza where a group of Indian and Spanish-American boys and girls had assembled. Red Feather spoke to the man in charge about the Hollisters entering the contests.

"Just the two older ones," he said. "No one under ten is running."

Pam was trailing.

"Say, this is fun," Pete said to Pam. "But I don't think we'll ever be able to beat the Indians."

"Let's try real hard, anyhow," his sister replied. "You know you're the best runner in your class at school, Pete."

The first race was to be a relay. A girl would run two laps around the market place, touch the hand of her partner and he would run three laps. When the man gave the signal, the girls lined up. Then he shouted:

"Go!"

Pam raced off with the other girls. One lap went by. Pam was trailing. On the second lap she lost even more ground before she touched her brother's 'hand. Pete ran as fast as he could, gradually catching up to the Indian runners.

"Come on, Pete!" Ricky shouted.

"You can beat 'em," Holly encouraged, jumping up and down in her excitement.

But as the race went into the fifth lap, Pete realized he could not keep up with the fleet native boys. When they crossed the finish line, Red Feather was first and Pete was last! But the Indian boy told him he had done very well.

"Now we will have a short race," the man said. "This will be once around the market place. The girls will start the race, run halfway, and touch the hands of the boys, who will finish."

He stationed the boys on one side of the square and the girls on the other.

"Win this one, Pete and Pam!" Ricky shouted, as everybody in the market place stopped to watch.

When the man shouted "Go!" Pam leaped forward with the speed of an antelope and took the lead. Two Indian girls and a pretty Spanish-American girl gained on her, but Pam stayed in first place halfway around the square. As she touched her brother's hand, Pete dashed off, his feet streaking over the hard-packed pavement.

Everybody was shouting, some for the Indians, some for the local children and still others for the Hollisters. Now Pete was five feet in the lead, but Red Feather was catching up on him.

"You can win it, Pete!" Holly yelled. "Don't let him pass you!"

With a final burst of speed Pete crossed the finish

line first as the onlookers sent up a rousing cheer for him and Pam.

"I'm so glad you won," Blue Feather said. "And you'll get prizes." She smiled. "They will help you remember us always."

The leader of the games presented each of the winners with moccasins. There was a pretty bead design on Pam's.

"They're beautiful," she said. "And now I guess we'd better go back to the hotel. It's lunch time." She put her arm around Blue Feather. "I love it here and I hope we'll see you again soon."

"Be sure to come to the pueblo tomorrow," Red Feather invited all the children. "There's to be a big celebration."

"Thanks. We will," Pete answered.

Pete crossed the finish line first.

The Hollisters returned to the hotel and had lunch with their parents. While they were eating, Pam handed her parents the unusual drinking vase, explaining what it was.

"It's a little early to give it to you," she said. "But I might break it if I keep it."

"Why this is a very attractive souvenir," her mother said. "Thank you all."

After everyone had rested an hour, Mr. Hollister said they would drive out to Juan Deer's *Chaparral* to see the articles he might buy.

"I just can't wait to see them," Holly spoke up. "Daddy, do you suppose I could have one tiny thing that the Indians made?"

"Like what?" her father smiled.

"A bracelet, maybe?" Holly asked.

"Why, I guess so. How about each of you children picking out one article—and Mother, too."

At three o'clock he brought the bus to the door and the family set off for Juan Deer's store. It was on a road little used now because of a new highway. As they drove up to the adobe building, the Hollisters saw a police car parked in front of it. As Mr. Hollister stopped the bus, a New Mexico state patrolman came from the store and walked up to him.

"I suppose you came to buy something," the officer said. "It's too bad, but there's nothing to sell. The place was cleaned out last night. Robbed!"

CHAPTER 11

The Silver Bracelets

THE HOLLISTERS could hardly believe what the policeman had just told them. After coming all this distance to buy the contents of The Chaparral— to find it had been robbed!

"I'd like to speak to Juan Deer, anyway," Mr. Hollister told the policeman and stepped into the store. His family followed.

What a sight met their eyes! Nothing but empty shelves and a few scattered pieces of paper and string. Everything had been taken out of the place.

But most pathetic of all was old Juan Deer himself. The old Indian stood mournfully in the middle of the floor, his head bowed. Seeing the Hollisters, he looked up questioningly.

"We're so sorry to hear about this, Mr. Deer," the children's father said after introducing himself and the others. "How did this happen?"

The Indian looked sadder than ever. "Place fixed up fine for Hollisters," he lamented. "Then all Indian things stolen by bad man. Policeman think he come in truck in middle of night."

"Yes, that's the theory," the officer spoke up. "I must report to headquarters now, Juan."

He went out and drove off.

"We'll try to help you find your things, Mr. Deer," Holly said kindly.

The Indian shook his head. "If thief have truck, everything many mile away by this time."

"That is sad," Mrs. Hollister remarked consolingly. "Indy Roades told us about the lovely things you had to sell."

"Indy write me about Hollisters," Juan Deer said, trying to smile. "He say many nice words. Yesterday a man come here. Say he buy everything. But I say wait for Hollisters. Now poor Juan Deer have nothing."

The children were touched by the man's plight. Who would have been so mean as to take everything he owned!

"We've solved some mysteries in Shoreham," Holly said. "Let's look for some clues!" she suggested to the others.

"We have to know what you lost, Mr. Deer," said Ricky.

The Indian pulled a piece of paper from his pocket. On it was written a list of what had been stolen.

"Oh, my goodness!" Mrs. Hollister exclaimed, as he read them off.

They included silver and turquoise pieces, pottery, vases, whole families of Indian dolls, moccasins, clothes and rugs. Juan Deer had no sooner put the paper back into his pocket when Holly came racing up to him.

"I found something," she said breathlessly. "This might be a clue, even if it is torn."

She held up half of a business card. The only thing printed on it was *oss*.

The old Indian patted Holly's head and said maybe the policeman would be glad to have it. He could not figure anything from it.

Mr. Hollister took the card and looked at it. "Juan Deer, don't you know anybody whose name ends in *oss?*" he asked.

As the shop keeper shook his head, Ricky came running into the store. He had been sleuthing outside and had found part of a torn card also.

"It was near the road!" he exclaimed.

His father found that the two pieces fitted together. The card read: *Dredmon Gross.*

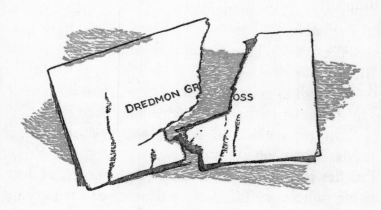

The two pieces fitted together.

Juan Deer put a finger to his forehead. "Oh yes. Mr. Gross the man who visit me yesterday to buy everything in store."

"Maybe he came back and robbed your store," Pete suggested.

At this moment they all heard a car coming along the road.

"If it's the policeman," Pam said, "we'd better tell him about the card."

But when the children hurried outside, it was not a police car that drew up. Instead it was a truck with a large brown canvas top. It pulled up in front of *The Chaparral* and a short, thin man stepped out. He had a long face and a slightly crooked nose. His mouth hardly moved as he spoke to Pete.

"Are you the Hollisters by any chance?"

"Yes, sir," Pete replied. "Do you know us?"

"No, but your father ruined my chance to buy the things in *The Chaparral*," he said.

"Oh, are you Mr. Gross?" Pam asked him.

"Yes. Why?"

"Did you drop a business card here last night?" Ricky put in.

"Of course not. What are you driving at?"

"The store was robbed," Holly explained.

Mr. Gross looked angry. "Are you trying to say I'm the thief?" he stormed.

No one answered this, as he went on, "If my card was found here, I must have dropped it yesterday.

Well, if there's nothing left, I'd better go shop some- where else."

"How do you know everything was taken?" Pete asked him. "We didn't say that."

Mr. Gross's face grew purple with rage. Muttering, he jumped out of the truck and went into the shop.

"I suppose he's going to tell Dad on us," Pete grinned.

"Say, this is a keen looking truck," Ricky said. "Let's look inside, Pete."

He pulled himself up and peeked through a flap in the canvas. Pete looked, too. Inside was a cot, a small chest of drawers and several suitcases.

"I guess he sleeps in here," Ricky remarked.

As the boy climbed inside, Sue said she wanted to look. Pete lifted her up and she too stepped into the truck.

"Oh, it's just like a bedroom," she said. "Let's play house, Ricky."

"Okay. What do you want to play?"

"We're on a trip," Sue replied. "It's getting to be night time. I'll go to bed—"

As she lay down on the cot, Pam peered in and said, "Better come out now. Mr. Gross—"

At this second the man burst from *The Chaparral*, looking as if he would like to eat somebody up.

"Get away from my truck!" he shouted at the children.

Ricky climbed down, but Sue was too frightened to move.

"Get away from my truck!"

"I'll help you," Pam whispered.

Sue reached out an arm. Before her sister could grab her, Mr. Gross pulled her from the truck and set her roughly on the ground.

"You stop!" Sue shrieked.

The commotion brought Mr. and Mrs. Hollister and Juan Deer from the shop.

"I'll thank you to keep your kids out of my truck hereafter!" Mr. Gross cried out.

He swung into the driver's seat, slammed the door and sped off. Pete looked after him, a scowl on his face.

"Dad, I don't think he's telling the truth about when he dropped that card," he said as the truck disappeared in a cloud of dust.

"The man may be perfectly innocent," Mr. Hollister said. "But Juan Deer will notify the police anyway."

"Well, that'll probably be the last we'll see of him," said Mrs. Hollister, "and I shan't be sorry."

As the Hollisters started for the bus, the Indian said again how sorry he was to have disappointed them.

"I try get you some things for *Trading Post* so trip be good," he said.

Suddenly he rolled up the sleeve which covered his right arm, revealing two beautiful silver bracelets, inlaid with turquoise. He turned to the children's mother.

"Juan Deer has not much to give," he said, "but these presents for two big girls. Will you let Juan Deer put them on arms?"

"How very nice of you!" Mrs. Hollister said. "But—"

The old Indian smiled as he slid them onto Pam's and Holly's wrists. "Maybe too big, but you can make smaller. Juan Deer feel sorry about long trip with bad ending. This make me feel better."

"Then we'll accept them, and thank you," Mrs. Hollister said.

The girls gazed at the beautiful gifts and then each of them kissed the kind old man.

"We'll take very good care of our bracelets," Pam told him as the Hollisters climbed into the bus.

They waved good-by and rode off, but all the way

back to Agua Verde they talked of nothing but the poor old Indian and the robbery. Mr. Hollister parked and they walked into the hotel. Swift Eagle who had been waiting for them arose from a sofa.

"I'm glad to see you again," he said. "I hope you've been enjoying yourselves."

Mr. Hollister told him about the robbery. Swift Eagle was shocked to hear it and said he surely hoped the police would catch the thief. After a little more conversation, he gave them an invitation to visit the pueblo.

"How would you like to come out there and see a real Indian corn dance tomorrow afternoon?"

"Oh goody!" Sue bubbled. "Does the corn dance like popcorn?"

Mr. Gross was talking secretly.

Swift Eagle laughed and explained that the corn dance was a prayer for rain to make the corn grow.

"You'll like it, I know," he added. "It means a lot to our people. We have not had much rain this summer, and our corn crop needs it badly."

He left them, saying he must get back to the pueblo. As soon as he had gone, Pam, Holly, and Ricky made a dash for the self-service elevator. Ever since arriving, Ricky had been wanting to run it himself with the others as passengers.

As the children neared it, they suddenly spotted Mr. Gross talking to a stout swarthy man behind a potted palm.

"I'll give you the money later, Rattler," Mr. Gross was saying.

Suddenly he looked up and saw the children. They thought he was coming after them, but instead he gave his friend a sidewise look and hurried to the street.

"I wonder what Mr. Gross was talking about?" Holly whispered as she stepped into the elevator with her brother and sister.

"Sh-hh!" Ricky said. "Here comes the other man."

Rattler stepped into the elevator with them, pushed the up button and the door slid shut. Then as the elevator started, he turned to the girls with flashing eyes and asked:

"Where did you get those bracelets?"

"Juan Deer gave them to us," Holly answered.

All the way to the second floor the man kept staring

at the silver and turquoise wristbands. Pam was frightened.

"Why is he looking at them so hard?" she thought.

The man was so interested in the jewelry that he barely noticed the elevator stop and the door quietly open. Pam pressed close to her sister and brother, relieved to know she would soon get away from the rude stranger.

As the Hollisters and Rattler stepped off the elevator, Pam's large bracelet slipped from her wrist onto the floor. The man stooped and snatched it up. But instead of handing it to the girl, he ran off with it.

"Stop!" Pam screamed.

"Stop! Stop!" the children shouted.

CHAPTER 12

The Corn Dance

"Stop! Stop!" the children shouted, chasing after the thief.

But the man took long leaping steps and reached the stairs well ahead of them. He rushed down, turned a sharp corner and dashed out a back door of the hotel. By the time the children reached the street, he was nowhere in sight.

"Oh, my pretty bracelet!" Pam cried out.

"We'd better tell Dad about this right away," Ricky said, turning back.

They found their parents in the lobby talking to the manager. When Pam burst out with her story, Mrs. Hollister exclaimed:

"How dreadful! We must do something at once!"

The manager grabbed his telephone and called the police. In a short time a state policeman arrived. Upon seeing the Hollisters he smiled, since he was the same one they had seen earlier at *The Chaparral*.

After introducing himself as Officer Martinez, he asked, "What happened? Another robbery?"

The children told him the details of the theft and

described the man whom Mr. Gross had called Rattler.

"I think I know who he is," Officer Martinez said. "A fellow who lives in the hills outside of town. He doesn't work much and sometimes he goes in for petty thievery."

"Please find him and get my beautiful bracelet back," Pam pleaded.

"I'll try," the officer promised. "If you should see him again, let me know immediately."

Pam felt so bad about the loss of the bracelet that she kept thinking about it all the next day. But at half past twelve, when the whole family was ready to set off for the Corn Dance, she put it from her mind.

The drive followed a winding stream between high rocky cliffs. The pueblo itself occupied a large flat meadow extending into the mountains. Fields of ripening Indian corn grew on all sides, and the entrance to the village was screened from view by a high adobe wall.

The visitors were met at the entrance by Swift Eagle and his grandchildren. A white dove was sitting on Blue Feather's shoulder and the girl stroked it as her grandfather greeted the Hollisters.

"Welcome to the land of the Yumatans!" the Indian governor said, smiling. "We live simply but we hope you will enjoy what we have to show you."

Turning toward the Indian children, he continued, "Red Feather and Blue Feather, will you guide your new young friends? I will show Mr. and Mrs. Hollister our pueblo."

Mrs. Hollister thought it best to keep Sue with her, but the others followed the Indian children. At once Pam asked them about the beautiful dove. Blue Feather said she had found it in the woods and trained the little pigeon to be a pet.

"Its name is Blanca," she said, leading the Hollister children inside the enclosure.

Before them, facing on a wide plaza, were many small, square buildings and a few low, round ones, all made of brown adobe. Presently the children came to a house with a green door.

"This is where we live," Blue Feather said. "Please come in."

"Oh no, that cane is never used."

The living room was scantily but comfortably furnished.

A bright colored Indian rug lay in the center of the earthen floor. A small table and three chairs stood near the door and a low adobe bench was built around two sides of the room. In a far corner was a low fireplace in which burned a small log of piñon wood.

"Um! How good that smells!" Pam said, sniffing the fragrant aroma.

Ricky was paying no attention to the rounded fireplace but was looking intently at the walls of the room. On one were several wooden pegs, from which hung beaded jewelry and wampum. On another was a black cane with a silver head.

"Does Swift Eagle have to walk with a cane sometimes?" Ricky asked, stepping closer to examine it.

Blue Feather shook her head. "Oh no," she said. "That cane is too important, and is passed on from governor to governor and never used."

"Why?" Holly chirped.

"See what it says on the head," the Indian boy pointed out proudly.

Pam went closer and read: "From Abraham Lincoln to the Governor of the Pueblo of the Yumatans."

Pete gasped. "From President Lincoln?"

"Yes," Blue Feather said. "When Abraham Lincoln was President, he invited all the Indian governors to Washington and presented them with canes."

They all climbed up.

After the Hollister children had taken a good look at the antique cane, Pete asked Blue Feather if they cooked their meals in the fireplace.

"Yes, and outside too. Come, I'll show you."

She led them to what looked like a tan-colored igloo. "This is our baking oven," the girl explained. "We share it with several other families to make bread and dry corn."

The Indian children led the Hollisters across the plaza toward a terraced cliff that towered at the rear of the reservation. Many caves were cut into the side of the rock, which could be reached only by a narrow trail and ladders.

"These are the old cliff dwellers' ruins," Red Feather said. "Our ancestors used to live up there."

The boy started up a long ladder which led to the

first terrace of the cliff dwellings. The others clambered after him. When they were safe on the first ledge, the Hollisters looked around. Far below them stood their parents with Sue and Swift Eagle. They waved to them.

"Can we climb up any higher?" Pete asked.

"Yes," Blue Feather answered. "Come on."

The Indian girl showed the way to another ladder which led to the next landing and they all climbed up.

"Here are the caves!" Ricky shouted. "I'd like to live in this big one."

The cavern, cut into the soft rock, was about the size of a small room in the Hollisters' home. Its floor was of hard clay, and the walls and ceiling were blackened by the smoke of ancient fires.

"Our ancestors lived very simply," Blue Feather said. "They cooked near the entrance and slept on blankets. All the water had to be carried up from a stream in the valley."

After the children had explored for awhile, Pete noticed a group of Indian boys far below, practicing with bows and arrows.

"Indy said we should learn how to shoot while we're here," Pete told Red Feather.

The Indian boy grinned. "We'll show you how."

He and his sister led the Hollisters down to a small field where the Yumatan children were practicing.

"What a funny target," Holly remarked, pointing

to a piece of wood in the ground at which they were aiming.

Three Indian boys were standing about twenty-five feet from it, taking turns. They did not miss once.

As the Indians ran forward to pull their arrows from the stick, Red Feather spoke to them in Tewa. In reply the archers smiled and handed their bows and arrows to the Hollister boys.

Pete's first arrow went wide of its mark, as did the second and third. Ricky had no better luck.

"Let me try," Pam said.

Several Indian girls standing nearby giggled when they saw Pam and Holly take their turns. Blue Feather quickly explained why.

"It's strange for them to see a girl shooting. Yuma-

"I guess this is a boy's game."

tan girls never touch a bow. We consider that a boy's game."

"Oh, it's fun!" Pam assured her, handing a bow in her direction. But the native girl smiled and shook her head no.

Pam and Holly tried again and again but could not hit the stake.

"I guess this is a boy's game," Pam sighed, as she and her sister gave up.

"We'll need a lot of practice to shoot like Indians," Pete laughed when the game was over.

Red and Blue Feather went back with the children to where Mr. and Mrs. Hollister and Sue were waiting with the Indian governor.

"My grandchildren and I must leave you now," Swift Eagle said. "We dress for the ceremony of the Corn Dance. It will start from the kiva."

He pointed to a round, flat adobe building located in the center of the plaza. A ladder stuck out from a hole in the top of it.

"What's a kiva?" Holly asked.

With a solemn expression Swift Eagle told them that the kiva was the center of the pueblo's religious life.

With that he hurried up the steps of the round building with Red and Blue Feather and disappeared down the ladder. As more Indians entered the kiva, the Spanish and Anglo visitors lined both sides of the plaza to watch the ceremony.

"Listen!" Pete said suddenly. "I hear drums!"

The Indians began to dance.

The sound of muffled drumbeats issued mysteriously from inside the kiva.

"Here they come!" Pam whispered excitedly.

A man carrying a long pole decorated with feathers and an embroidered banner came up the ladder, followed by a chorus of gaily dressed braves. They wore red, white and green velvet shirts and many strings of silver, wampum and coral necklaces. Their calico trousers were made of multi-colored prints.

"Oh look!" Holly said. "The men wear earrings!"

When the chanters reached the ground, drummers appeared beating tom-toms. Next came the procession of dancers in two long lines, with men and women alternating. Following them were boys and girls arranged according to size.

"Those cute little ones at the end of the line are

only about two years old," Mrs. Hollister said in amazement.

Never before had the Hollisters seen such beautiful costumes. The men wore white embroidered kilts, fox tails down their backs, skunk fur leg bands and moccasins. Their hair hung over their shoulders and in their hands they carried gourd rattles and evergreen boughs.

The women wore black dresses fastened over one shoulder and tied with a woven sash about the waist. They too had beautiful jewelry and carried pine boughs. But what interested the Hollisters most was the women's headdresses. Their hair hung loose and on their heads they wore wooden boards painted in turquoise color.

"Aren't they lovely?" Mrs. Hollister said.

As the drumbeats became louder, the Indians began to dance. They leaned forward, hopping up and down in perfect rhythm to the drums. Then they formed circles, and after that danced to the North, East, South and West, praying for rain in all directions to make their corn grow tall.

"I don't see Red and Blue Feather," Pam said anxiously. "Why aren't they dancing?"

The answer came soon afterward when the Indian dancers retreated into the kiva and another group replaced them. Among them were Red and Blue Feather.

Suddenly the Hollisters were startled by two weird-looking figures who dashed from the kiva and raced in and out among the dancers. Their bodies were painted black with white stripes and polka dots. The men's hair was plastered up into topknots, finished off with bits of feather and corn husks. And they wore little black aprons front and back, which flipped up and down as they pranced around.

"Yikes! That's the kind of ghost I want to be on Halloween!" Ricky exclaimed. "What are they, Dad?"

Mr. Hollister said that Swift Eagle had told him about these funny men. They were called Koshari, and pretended to come out of the spirit world to tease the dancers.

After the Indians had danced a long while, they started back for the kiva. Holly had been so intent watching that she did not turn when she felt a hand on her left arm.

"Yes, Pete," she said vaguely, knowing he was next to her. When he did not answer, the girl looked around. Her brother was paying no attention. Then Holly quickly glanced down at her wrist. The silver and turquoise bracelet was gone! In a panic she nudged Pete.

"My bracelet's been stolen!" she whispered. "Somebody just took it off my arm. Let's find him!"

The children broke away from the group and looked about. Suddenly Holly pointed.

"See that man climbing the ladder on the cliff! He looks like Rattler. I'll bet he's the one!"

"Let's get him!" Pete whispered.

CHAPTER 13

A Strange Story

"How shall we catch him?" Holly asked Pete, as the shadowy figure climbed higher on the ladder.

The boy did not want to disturb the ceremony to ask for help and his parents had moved several yards away. By the time they understood what was wanted of them, the thief would be gone.

"I'll go after him myself," Pete said.

"Oh, you mustn't!" Holly cried out fearfully.

Two Indian men standing off at a little distance heard her and turned around. Quickly Pete ran up to them and asked:

"Will you help us catch a thief?"

"Where is he?"

Pete pointed and immediately they raced off with the two Hollisters. When they reached the ladder, the man was nearly up to the first terrace.

"Come down here!" Pete cried out.

The man stopped a moment and glanced down, then started up again.

"Do as the boy says!" one of the Indians shouted sternly.

At this command the climber halted, then came

down. When he arrived at the bottom, Pete and Holly gasped. The man was not Rattler at all, but Mr. Gross!

"You Hollister kids again!" he sneered. "What ails you?"

"I—I thought you stole my bracelet," Holly said, looking questioningly at him.

"Your bracelet? What are you talking about?" the man asked. He wheeled toward the two Indians. "Next time don't listen to these kids," he warned them and started to walk away.

But Pete stepped in front of him. "We've been looking for you to ask if you know where the man named Rattler is."

"Rattler? I don't know anybody by the name of Rattler," Mr. Gross snarled.

"What ails you Hollister kids?"

"You were talking to him in our hotel," Holly said. "Right after that he took my sister Pam's bracelet."

Mr. Gross gave an ugly laugh. "I remember now. He's just a beggar. He asked me for money but I wouldn't give him a cent. I don't know anything about him."

Mr. Gross strode away, leaving Pete and Holly open-mouthed with the two Indians. The men shrugged and went back. In a few minutes the children rejoined their parents and told what had happened.

"It's very strange," said Mr. Hollister. "Why was the thief or thieves so eager to get hold of those particular bracelets?"

"Maybe it was because they had belonged to Juan Deer," Pam suggested.

"Possibly," her father agreed. "But I'm more inclined to think the bracelets may have some special significance."

"What's that?" Sue asked.

"Well, some things have special meaning or value to certain people," he explained. "Just what did the bracelets look like?"

Pam said hers had a greenish blue turquoise and that the design was not like any she had seen before on Indian jewelry. It consisted of two coyote heads peeking out from some leaves.

"Mine was like that too," said Holly, "and crossed arrows sort of mixed in with them."

"They both have leaves and they both have green-

"Mr. Gross and Rattler are in cahoots."

ish blue turquoise," Pete reflected. "Perhaps the thief is looking for a bracelet with one or the other for some reason."

"Well, I don't care what the reason is," said Holly. "I want my bracelet back!"

"I want mine too," Pam added. "Say, do you suppose the special bracelet could have anything to do with the lost mine?"

"How could it?" Pete asked and Pam had no answer.

Before the Hollisters left the pueblo they told Swift Eagle how much they had enjoyed their visit but also explained what had happened. He promised to inquire among the Indians, but was sure none of the Yumatans had stolen the bracelet.

"I guess we'll never see our jewelry again," Holly sighed as they walked to their bus.

They continued to talk about the loss all the next day. As the family was finishing lunch, Pete said suddenly:

"I believe Mr. Gross and Rattler are in cahoots."

"In where?" Sue asked innocently.

"I mean I think they're up to something together," her brother replied, smiling. "Don't you remember, Pam, you said you overheard Mr. Gross say, 'I'll give you the money later, Rattler'? That doesn't sound as if he didn't know Rattler."

"You're right," Mr. Hollister agreed.

"Then shouldn't we tell the police about Holly's bracelet?" Pete suggested.

"Yes. Phone them, will you?" he asked and then followed his wife upstairs.

While the boy was gone, Swift Eagle came into the hotel looking for the Hollister children. He carried a covered basket and when Pete returned, the governor smiled and said:

"Pam and Holly, your friends Red Feather and Blue Feather felt so bad about the stolen bracelets that they asked me to bring you something in place of them. And, of course, I couldn't forget you other children."

"This is very 'citing," said Sue, standing close to him as he seated himself in a lounging chair.

He opened the basket and handed each of them a small package. The girls opened theirs first. The ohs and ahs which followed sounded just like Christmas morning in the Hollister house.

"A beautiful new bracelet!" Pam said, as she tried on the lovely silver and turquoise gift. "Oh thank you so much!"

Holly squealed with delight when she saw one for herself, and Sue had a very small special bracelet which looked older than the others.

"This one has been owned by my people many years," Swift Eagle explained.

Pam said Sue must take extra good care of it.

"I will. I'll love it with my whole life," Sue replied, touching it to her cheek.

All the bracelets were more ornate than the ones that had been stolen. The silver work was scrolled in lovely cloud designs, and the turquoise inlays were the most beautiful they had ever seen.

"And here are packages for the boys," Swift Eagle said.

"And here are packages for the boys."

When Ricky opened his gift he warwhooped, "Bow and arrow! This is a honey!"

He held up a miniature silver bow and a tiny arrow for the others to see.

"And it has a real bowstring, too!" Ricky exclaimed gleefully.

He fitted the nock of the arrow into the string and sent the little arrow flying a few feet.

"What did you get, Pete?" Holly asked.

Pete grinned as he pulled out a small silver eagle. "Hey, what's this between the eagle's claws?" he asked, looking up at the governor.

"Examine it yourself," the Indian challenged him, and Pete pulled a long silver stick from the clenched claws. "Oh, it's a pencil!" the boy declared. He turned the top and the lead poked out of the other end. "This is nifty!"

"You can write cards to your friends back home," Pam suggested.

"I'll do it right away!" Pete grinned.

He thanked Swift Eagle and hurried over to the hotel desk, where he bought postcards showing scenes of the Yumatan country. He would send them to Dave Mead and some of the other fellows back in Shoreham.

Ricky meanwhile took his miniature bow and arrow and hurried to the garden of the hotel. He noticed a horned toad near a clump of cactus. The boy whistled and stomped. When the toad did not move he decided it was only a life-like figure of one.

"I'll pretend to shoot him," Ricky told himself. "I'm a big game hunter!"

He aimed his arrow and let fly. It landed in the sandy soil directly back of the toad. Then, to the boy's utter astonishment, the toad quivered and hopped into some rabbit brush!

"Oh!" Ricky gasped. "He's alive! Am I glad I didn't hit him!"

Back in the hotel lobby Pam, Holly and Sue stood talking with Swift Eagle and admiring their new bracelets.

"This time nobody is going to take mine from me!" Holly said determinedly, looking up at the kind Indian.

"Will you tell us how they're made?" Pam asked as she turned her bracelet over and over in the palm of her hand.

"Of course," the Indian said, pleased that the girls were enjoying their gifts.

He told how Indian silversmiths first pound out strips of silver. Then they use small hammers and chisels to cut the settings. "These have to be done perfectly so that the turquoise stones will not fall out," Swift Eagle said.

He had no sooner said this than Sue exclaimed, "Oh, mine came out!"

The lovely turquoise stone had fallen to the floor. As Sue bent down to pick it up, Swift Eagle said:

"I guess this bracelet is so old that the setting is worn. But I'll repair it for you."

He held out his hand and Sue put the bracelet and turquoise into it. As the Indian examined them, he said:

"You know there's an old legend that Indians used to send secret messages under the turquoise stones."

"Really?" the question came from Pete, who had just returned from writing his cards and dropping them in the mailbox. "Were the messages in code?"

Swift Eagle said he thought they must have been because there was not enough room underneath the turquoise to write much.

Suddenly Pam's eyes grew wide and she looked at her brother eagerly. "Oh Pete, could it be that—?"

"You mean, the stolen bracelets?" he said excitedly.

"Exactly!" Pam replied. "Maybe the bracelet thief is looking for a message beneath some turquoise stone!"

"We must speak in private."

Swift Eagle smiled at them. "Two real detectives, I can see that," he said in praise. "The secret messages I told you about were used by ancient Indians. I have never heard of the practice in modern times."

"Just the same," Pam said, "people *could* still send messages that way. Do you suppose that the thief wanted the bracelets from *The Chaparral* so he could look for a message?"

"You surely are busy putting your clues together," Swift Eagle remarked. "And look," he added, pointing to the door, "here comes Officer Martinez. You might tell him how you've figured things out."

The policeman approached, looking very serious. He merely nodded at the children and said: "Swift Eagle, I'd like to speak to you."

"What is it?" the governor asked him.

"We must speak in private," the patrolman added.

Swift Eagle left the children and walked to the corner of the lobby with the policeman. In a few minutes he came back, a frown of worry on his face.

Swift Eagle was so upset he could hardly talk. "I had planned to entertain you and your parents this afternoon," he said. "But now I won't be able to."

"Has something terrible happened?"

"Yes, I'm afraid it has," the Indian replied. "I must go with the policeman."

"Why?" Pete asked.

"One of the rugs stolen from *The Chaparral*," the governor said, "has been found near my pueblo! The Yumatans are being blamed for the robbery!"

CHAPTER 14

Galloping Messengers

"Do THEY think your nice Indians stole the rug?" Holly asked Swift Eagle in bewilderment.

The governor looked grave. "Since I am head of my tribe," he said, "I will have to answer for the charge."

"They can't do that!" Holly said, grasping one of Swift Eagle's hands. She looked up pleadingly at the policeman. "You won't take him away, will you, Mr. Martinez?"

The patrolman said he was just as sad about the whole thing as the children were, but that Swift Eagle would have to go to headquarters until it was known for sure that no one in the pueblo had stolen the rug and other articles from *The Chaparral*. As they left the hotel, Holly and Sue burst into tears.

"Don't cry," Pam said, putting her arms around them. "There's certainly some mistake and we're going to find out what it is!"

"You bet we are," Pete cried.

The children ran upstairs to tell their mother and father what had happened.

"Oh, I'm so sorry," Mrs. Hollister sighed.

137

"Elaine, we're going to have to do something for Swift Eagle," Mr. Hollister said. "Let's drive out to the pueblo and see how we can help."

Holly wiped her eyes when she heard this. As they hurried off in the bus, Pete said he wondered whether the rug was really one that had been in Juan Deer's shop.

"You mean it might only look like the stolen one?" Ricky asked.

"Yes."

"Or somebody could have put it there on purpose to make the Indians look guilty?" Pam reasoned.

"How could anybody be so mean?" Holly burst out.

After Mr. Hollister had driven the bus for about twenty minutes, he said, "This territory doesn't look familiar. I believe I'm on the wrong road."

"I think you did take the wrong fork half a mile back," Mrs. Hollister replied. "The road to the pueblo wasn't so rough."

Her husband was just about to turn the bus around when he noticed a truck parked up ahead at a small thicket of cedars and piñon bushes.

"That looks familiar," he said. "Wasn't Mr. Gross's truck a brown covered one?"

"Yes," Pete answered. "Let's drive a little closer. Maybe Rattler's with him!"

Mr. Hollister drove ahead. The truck was indeed the one Mr. Gross had been driving but the front seat was empty.

"What is it?" Pete asked.

"Perhaps he ran out of gas and had to walk back to town," Pete suggested.

Ricky jumped out. "Maybe he's in the back." Climbing into the cab, the boy lifted the flap to the rear and looked in.

"No, Mr. Gross isn't here," Ricky called, "or Mr. Rattler either. But, say, I see a box like I saw at Indy's. It might've come from *The Chaparral!*"

Hearing this, everyone got out of the bus. Pete also pulled himself up to the driver's seat and looked into the dim interior.

"What is it?" he asked his brother.

Ricky was making his way to the rear. On the floor lay a large carved box for holding jewelry and trinkets. As the boy reached down, he suddenly screamed.

"Ow! Ouch!" He pulled back quickly.

"What's the matter?" Pete asked, leaping to the back of the truck. A second later he shouted, "A snake!"

Ricky and Pete jumped out of the truck in a hurry, with Ricky waving his hand in pain. His mother and father asked what the trouble was.

"A snake bit me here," Ricky said, holding his right hand up gingerly.

"Oh dear," Mrs. Hollister said. "John, look at the snake and see if it's poisonous."

Mr. Hollister ran to the back of the truck, pulled aside the flap and glanced inside. Coiled on the floor was a large bull snake.

"Thank goodness it's harmless," he reported.

Everybody was relieved to know that Ricky had not been poisoned. Nevertheless his thumb was sore so Mrs. Hollister took the first aid kit from the bus and put salve on her son's hand.

"Do you think Mr. Gross keeps that snake in his truck on purpose?" Pam asked.

"You mean to scare people who get in?" Holly asked.

"Yes."

"It might have crawled in from the desert," Mr. Hollister ventured. "Well, we can soon find out," he added. "Here comes Mr. Gross now."

The tourist was scrambling over some rocks and buffalo grass as fast as he could. Getting nearer, he called out:

"I thought I heard voices. Who—?" Suddenly he

recognized the Hollisters. "What are you doing around my truck?" he stormed.

"We were looking for you," Mr. Hollister replied. "And by the way, Ricky was bitten by a snake in your truck."

"Serves him right. He had no business snooping!" the man went on angrily. "He shouldn't have opened that box."

"But I didn't open the box," Ricky insisted.

"You must have," the man said gruffly, "or else the snake wouldn't have bitten you."

"I'm sure my son is telling the truth," his father said, looking hard at Mr. Gross. "And, as long as you're here, we want to ask you some questions. Even though you deny knowing the fellow you called Rattler, we think you can tell us more about him."

"Well, I can't," denied Mr. Gross, getting into his truck.

"What were you doing out here?" Pete asked him.

The man seemed to be taken aback by the sudden question. "Why-uh—I was looking for rock plants."

He started the motor and raced off in a cloud of dust.

"That man is the rudest person I've ever met," Mrs. Hollister said.

They returned to their bus and Mr. Hollister backed it around. He found the right road to the pueblo and in a short time arrived at the Yumatans' home. They were met by Red Feather and Blue Feather, who saw the bus coming in.

"Did you see my grandfather in town?" Red Feather asked as the Hollisters alighted.

"Yes, they did," his sister answered for them, glancing at Pam's and Holly's wrists. "The girls are wearing their surprises."

"The bracelets are beautiful," Pam said but she did not sound gay. She was trying to hide her sorrow about the Yumatans being in trouble because of the stolen rug.

"And my silver bow and arrows are keen," Ricky went on but without his usual enthusiasm.

By this time the Indians sensed that something was wrong. Blue Feather cocked her head to one side.

"Why aren't the Hollisters happy?" she asked.

Mr. Hollister could not keep the story from the

"Did you see my grandfather?"

children any longer, especially since Holly looked as if she were about to burst into tears. He quickly told the Indians what had happened. But although their eyes became moist, they did not cry.

"Yumatans are not thieves," Blue Feather said indignantly, her lower lip quivering.

"I'm going to tell Mr. Martinez so," her brother blurted out, and started to move off.

"Wait!" Mr. Hollister called to him. "Perhaps we can find a clue that will convince the police your people are not to blame."

Red Feather looked up sorrowfully at Mr. Hollister. "What can we do?"

"Who is next in command to Swift Eagle?" Mr. Hollister asked.

Blue Feather brightened a little when she heard this. "His lieutenant, Po-da," she replied. "He is very old and very wise."

"Will you take us to him?" Mr. Hollister asked.

"Yes. Follow us," the Indian boy replied, beckoning to them.

He hurried along in the lead, with the others following him and his sister to a small hut with a red door.

"Po-da!" the boy called out. "There is trouble for the Yumatans. Please come out and help us."

A moment later a wrinkled old man stepped from the hut. He wore blue pants and a bright red shirt. Around his waist was a white blanket with blue stripes.

Po-da called the tribe.

When he saw the Hollisters he bowed politely, then asked Red Feather, "What is this trouble of Yumatans?"

After introducing the Hollisters in English, Red Feather spoke to the old man rapidly in Tewa. The children watched Po-da's face to see how he would take the bad news. But the wise Indian did not change his stolid expression. Instead he shuffled into the house and came out with a small drum. Climbing some steps to the roof of his house, he beat the drum with a throbbing *boom-da-boom.*

The Hollisters could hardly believe their eyes, for as if by magic everybody in the pueblo became quiet. Children stopped playing. Women ceased their activities, and the men put down their handicraft.

Swiftly they gathered in a big circle below Po-da, murmuring questions.

The old man held up his arms for silence. Speaking slowly and gesturing, he told them in their native tongue. A great shout of anger went up from the people. Po-da silenced them again and continued speaking the strange words.

Pete nudged Red Feather. "What is he saying?" the boy whispered.

"He's asking if anybody saw a person around here with a stolen rug."

Suddenly a man cried out a reply, and Red Feather explained, "He says he saw a stranger sneaking around near the pueblo with a bundle under his arm."

"That was the real thief!" Pam said excitedly.

"And I'll bet a cookie it was Rattler!" Pete reasoned. "The police should question him!"

Before the children could say more, the lieutenant-governor sent Red Feather and his sister off on an errand. Then he began to speak in English.

"Mr. and Mrs. Hollister," he said, "Yumatans not recognize person who come and put rug near pueblo. Maybe disguised. Po-da send message to Patrolman Martinez."

"I'll take the message to him!" Mr. Hollister offered.

"Thank you, no!" Po-da bowed. "Indians have own short cut to village."

As he finished, the Hollisters could hear the clatter of hoofs and a moment later the Indian children

145

They thundered along the secret trail.

led two spirited horses up to the old man. His eyes squinted against the sun as he surveyed the throng of Yumatans before him. Then he shouted:

"Sharp Wind! Running Flame!"

Two braves ran forward.

"Go!"

Not even taking time to saddle up, the Yumatan riders flung themselves onto the horses' backs. Then as the tribe cheered they thundered off along their secret trail toward the village.

CHAPTER 15

A Jolly Drum Maker

THE TWO Indian riders disappeared over a rocky ridge as the Yumatans watched in silence. When the hoof-beats could be heard no longer, Po-da climbed down from the roof and turned to Mr. Hollister.

"Thank you for bringing message," he said with a faint smile. "Sharp Wind and Running Flame best riders of tribe. Tell police quick. Swift Eagle come back."

Then Po-da told his people to return to their work and the meeting broke up.

"Those horses are super," Pete said to Red Feather. "Can you ride like that?"

The Indian boy said that all Yumatan children learn to ride as soon as they are old enough to sit on a pony.

"We keep the children's ponies in a corral at the edge of the pueblo," his twin added. "Would you like to see them?"

"May I ride one?" Ricky burst out eagerly.

"If you know how."

"I can ride a little."

It was decided that Pete, Pam and Holly would

take turns also and they set off with their Indian friends.

"What a strange-looking corral!" Pete thought. Instead of a board fence it was enclosed with cedar posts.

"We keep our sheep in here, too," Red Feather said, opening a low gate.

As his sister closed it behind them, the Hollisters saw that the corral contained several sheep and a number of pinto ponies. Two of the ponies came up to the Indians.

"We call them Sun and Moon," Blue Feather explained, patting the ponies. "Sun has the brown spots and Moon the black ones."

"Can we ride 'em bareback like the braves did?" Pete queried.

"We call them Sun and Moon."

"Try it. We do," Red Feather answered.

With a little struggling, Pete and Pam climbed to the ponies' backs and trotted out of the corral into a fenced-in field.

"This is dreamy," Pam giggled, "but a little slippery to stay on."

After the children had made several circles Ricky and Holly asked for turns. The older children hopped off. They boosted Ricky onto Sun and Holly onto Moon.

"I'm an Indian!" Ricky shouted and gave a whoop.

"Don't frighten the ponies!" Blue Feather warned him.

But Sun already had become nervous. He ran faster, with Ricky clinging to his mane.

"Stop!" the frightened boy shouted.

But Sun only raced faster. Suddenly Blue Feather cried out a command in Tewa. Sun stopped short, throwing Ricky right over his head.

As Pam screamed, her young brother somersaulted and landed in a piñon bush. But he jumped up unhurt and the others cheered.

"We'd better go back now," Pam said.

The Hollisters found their parents and Sue standing near one of the oval outdoor ovens eating fresh baked wheat bread and rabbit stew out of aspenwood bowls.

"It's 'licious," Sue said between bites.

"You eat some, too," said a stout Indian woman who was tending the oven, smiling at the newcomers.

Pam thought she looked very attractive in her green skirt, purple blanket and white boots.

"Thank you," they said, taking the hot food she offered.

As they finished eating, the Hollisters heard a great shout at the entrance to the pueblo. Through the gate rode Swift Eagle in his truck, followed by Sharp Wind and Running Flame on their horses.

The governor drove up to where the Hollisters were standing and hopped out. How Red and Blue Feather hugged him!

As the other Indians gathered and cheered, Swift Eagle said that the Yumatans were no longer blamed for the theft and he thanked the Hollisters for their help. In a few minutes his people went back to their various tasks.

Even Blanca seemed to know everybody was happy. The dove, which had been fluttering about, landed on Pam's shoulder and kissed her. The Indians laughed.

"Blanca like Anglo children," came a voice from nearby.

The Hollisters turned to see a broad-faced Indian sitting on a blanket in front of his house. He held a half-finished drum between his legs. Others of all sizes lay around him.

"That's Jemez the drum maker," said Red Feather, leading the visitors over and introducing them to him. "He's the jolliest man in our pueblo and is full of jokes."

"See, it'll hold me," Holly cried.

"May we look at your things?" Pete asked him politely.

Jemez nodded and said if they wanted to they might beat upon them.

"Are these the same kind of drums that Santa Claus brings at Christmas?" Ricky asked, turning a turquoise and white one over in his hands.

Jemez shook his head no. "These ceremonial drum," he said. "Very strong aspen wood and rawhide. No break."

"You mean you can jump on them?" Holly asked impishly.

Jemez looked up and grinned. Blue Feather held one hand over her mouth to smother a giggle.

"You can jump on big drum over there," the man said, pointing to a giant instrument nearly as tall as

Holly. Pete and Pam boosted her to the top of it.

"See, it'll hold me," Holly cried in delight as she jumped on the middle of it. Then suddenly she gasped.

Crash! The little girl went right through the drum!

Although the Hollisters had not noticed, several children had been watching Holly and they all laughed.

"It's one of Jemez' jokes," Blue Feather told Holly, who by this time had recovered from her surprise. "Many Anglo children like to stand on drums, so Jemez has a special one with a cardboard top which they fall through."

Mr. and Mrs. Hollister and Red Feather joined the amused onlookers in time to see Holly climb out of the drum. Jemez set about immediately putting a new paper top on it so as to be ready for the next curious visitor.

"I believe we should leave now," Mrs. Hollister said, but the children begged for more time to play around the pueblo.

"Please," Ricky said, "we're having such a good time."

When Sue saw that her mother was not inclined to give permission, she suddenly chirped, "Everybody who loves Mommy put up his right hand!"

All within hearing laughed and shot his right hand into the air. Mrs. Hollister blushed with happy embarrassment.

"You little monkey," she said, kissing her small

daughter. "All right. You may all stay a while longer."

"How about practicing some more with the bows and arrows?" Red Feather suggested.

"I'd like that," Pete answered.

"Me too," said Ricky.

"I guess not," Pam said, recalling that Indian girls never become archers. She thought it might not be very polite to try shooting again while in the pueblo.

Holly felt the same way and besides she did not want the Indians to laugh at her again. "I'll wait till I get home," she said.

Red Feather led Pete and Ricky to where several of his friends had gathered with their archery outfits.

"Suppose we shoot at a moving target this time," the Indian boy suggested.

The Indian boys took turns.

"Like skeet shooting?" Pete asked. "My Dad and I have done that."

When Red Feather said the Indians did not know what this meant, Pete told them that skeet shooting is firing shots at flying clay pigeons.

"We play that kind of game, too," Red Feather said, "only we shoot with bows and arrows. And instead of clay pigeons, we use a ball covered with feathers."

The Indian boys took turns showing the Hollisters how they could hit the feathery target. This was not so easy for them as shooting at the stick on the ground but they did pretty well.

When it was Ricky's turn, he missed on the first six tries but sent the arrow into the ball the next time.

"Now let's see how you make out," Red Feather said to Pete, handing him a bow and arrow.

Red Feather tossed the ball into the air and Pete's arrow flew straight at it.

"A hit!" Ricky shouted.

"Anglo boy is a good shot," one of the Yumatan boys said admiringly.

"I'm just lucky," Pete grinned and hoped he would hit the next ball.

Zing! Plop! He hit it again.

Pete was then matched against Red Feather and two other Indian boys. The contest was close, but Pete's practice at skeet shooting was in his favor and he won.

"He's a champ!" Ricky cried gleefully and re-

"Let's go in the direction Mr. Gross came from."

peated this to his family and Blue Feather as they walked up.

"Good for you!" Mr. Hollister praised his son.

He said they must leave the pueblo now. Red and Blue Feather walked back to the bus with them and waved as the Hollisters drove off.

"Didn't we have fun?" Sue said enthusiastically.

"We sure did," Pete laughed. Then leaning toward his father, he added, "Dad, take that wrong road again, will you? I'd like to see whether Mr. Gross came back. If he did, I want to find out what he's doing."

"Yes," said Pam. "Rattler might be hiding there."

"All right, detectives," their father replied.

When he reached the fork, he turned up the bumpy road to the place where Ricky had been nipped by the snake. Mr. Gross's truck was not there.

"Let's look around, anyway," Pete suggested. "Maybe we'll pick up a clue."

"You mean to the turquoise mine?" Ricky asked, as they all scrambled out of the bus.

"Let's go in the direction Mr. Gross came from," Pam said, running across the rocks through the low brush. The others followed her.

After they had gone some distance the Hollisters noticed that the ground began to rise. The way was strewn with small boulders, and tall brush slowed their progress.

Suddenly Pam, some fifty feet ahead, stopped short. Before her was a breathtaking view.

"Hurry, everybody!" she called.

As Pete, Holly, and Ricky reached her side, Pam pointed to a deep canyon below them.

"Don't get too close to the edge," she warned. "It drops right off."

"What's that stone tower over there?" Ricky pointed to his left. "Let's see."

The four started off with Pam in the lead. But she had gone forward only a few feet when suddenly she screamed and disappeared!

CHAPTER 16

An Ancient Hide-out

THE HOLLISTER children stood stunned for a couple of seconds after Pam had vanished. Then they hurried forward to where they had last seen her. There was a deep cleft in the rocks which ran at right angles to the cliff.

Looking down a short distance, Pete saw to his relief that his sister had only slipped feet first part way down the wedge-shaped cut. Her shoulders were propped against one side, her feet on the other.

"Pam, are you all right?" he called.

"I—I guess so," she replied breathlessly. "My elbows and knees are skinned. But how am I going to get out of here?"

The other children, meanwhile, had raced back frantically to get their parents, who came as fast as they could.

"If we only had a rope to throw down to you!" Mrs. Hollister exclaimed anxiously.

"I see something," the girl cried out excitedly.

She had noticed an opening in the cleft a few feet below her. Inching down like a caterpillar by way of some natural hand and toe holds in the rocky sides, she reached the entrance to a cave and stepped into it.

"Mother! Daddy!" she called up, "The other side of this cave looks out over the valley. It's an old Indian cliff dwelling!"

"What a discovery!" Mr. Hollister said in surprise, "You'll have to stay down there, Pam, until I go for help."

Ricky, who until now had watched wide-eyed at Pam's plight, shouted, "Yikes! This'll be a real cliff rescue just like in the movies. Come on, men, let's find a rope."

When Pam heard this, she looked up through the crevice. "Don't worry about me. I'll be all right," she said bravely. "Dad, before you go for a rope, let me look around here. I can see a terrace and more caves. Maybe I'll find some way to climb out."

"All right. But be careful," her father warned.

"Look out for snakes!" Ricky cried.

"And bears," Sue called.

Pam began her search through the gloomy interior of the old cliff dwelling. The first room was bare. Walking carefully, she stepped through a low doorway into the next one. It, too, was empty and there were no openings or steps for her to climb to the top of the cliff.

"Oh dear!" the girl sighed, discouraged.

As she went in and out along the rocky terrace and from room to room of the ancient Indian dwelling, Pam found that some of the rooms were set deep into the mountain. She was careful to note where she was

Pam began her search through the interior.

going in order to find her way back. Once she stopped to gaze at the lofty tower which rose from the terrace and extended high above the cliff top.

"How wonderful all this is!" the girl told herself, gazing down on the terraces and valley below.

A few terraces had big round rooms without roofs, which she recognized as the ruins of kivas. Pam became so interested that she almost forgot she was looking for a way to get out.

"I wonder what those ancient Indians did in these rooms," the girl asked herself.

Seeing an old oblong stone with a groove worn into the top of it, Pam guessed that this was an ancient corn grinder. Suddenly she remembered her anxious family and started running through the other rooms.

"Lots of people must have lived here," Pam thought, then stopped short.

She was in a large kiva, on the floor of which lay a ladder.

"Oh! Now I can get out!" Pam cried aloud.

She picked up one end of the ladder and dragged it to the opening in the cleft. It was not until Pam was halfway up that a startling thought came to her.

"It's a new ladder! How did it ever get here?"

The girl's heart began to thump. Maybe she had found Rattler's hide-out!

Reaching the top of the crevice, Pam climbed out and ran into her mother's outstretched arms.

"You're safe!" Mrs. Hollister cried. "Oh, how thankful I am!"

"Mother! Dad!" Pam said excitedly. "I found the ladder in a kiva—and it's a new one! It might belong to Rattler and this is his secret home!"

"Oh!" Holly exclaimed. "Maybe he hid our bracelets down there."

"I certainly think we should explore this place," Mr. Hollister said. "It would be an ideal spot to hide stolen goods."

"Yikes!" Ricky shouted. "Maybe we'll solve the mystery of *The Chaparral* and find all Juan Deer's things!"

"Don't raise your hopes too high," his mother warned him.

The Hollisters went down the ladder one by one.

When they reached the bottom, the family looked about the gloomy ruins.

"It's kind of spooky," Sue said, holding tightly to her mother's hand.

There was not a sound except the hollow echo of her voice.

"If Rattler's here, he's well hidden," Pam whispered.

"Let's start hunting," Pete urged.

"But we'll stay together," his father said.

After walking through the rooms and seeing nothing, Pete suggested that they take the ladder and hunt in the dwellings on the next terraces below. Mr. Hollister consented but said only he and Pete would go.

The two worked their way up and down the terraces and in and out of the kivas. They could find

"It's kind of spooky."

nothing but a few broken pieces of ancient pottery; not a sign of a person.

"Well, I guess we were wrong about anybody hiding stolen goods here," Pete said.

They made their way back to the topmost row of apartments and reported their disappointment to the others. The ladder was set up again in the crevice and Mrs. Hollister was about to start the climb, when Pam called:

"I've found another room, way back under the ground."

In a corner near where she was standing, Pam had noticed a small opening. As she crawled through it, she cried out in surprise.

"There's a lot of stuff piled up in here!"

Quickly the others got down on hands and knees and pulled themselves into the room. It was so dim that they could see practically nothing.

"I'll light a match," Mr. Hollister said, taking a book of them from his pocket.

As the tiny flame flickered, everybody gasped in amazement. The room was filled with silver and turquoise jewelry, pottery, moccasins, rugs and Indian clothing.

"From *The Chaparral!*" Pete exclaimed. "Here's a tag. It says *The Chaparral!*"

As their father lit another match, the children hurried over to examine the articles. Among the stolen merchandise was a set of tin candlesticks and some candles in a box. Mr. Hollister set them up and

"Here are the bracelets Juan Deer gave us!"

lighted the candles. At once Pam and Holly dropped to their knees to examine several bracelets that were lying on the floor.

"The stones have been taken out of them!" Holly said sadly. Then she exclaimed, "Oh, here are the turquoises," and picked up a small box in which the beautiful blue-green gems had been placed.

"And look, every bracelet has a leaf design," Pam said. "Now I know that design means something, because Blue Feather says most of their jewelry has a cloud or raindrop pattern."

Holly suddenly squealed in amazement. "Pam, here are the bracelets Juan Deer gave you and me!"

Before them lay the pieces of jewelry with the coyote heads and the crossed arrows.

"That proves Rattler is the thief," Pete stated.

"You're right, son," Mr. Hollister agreed. "And

all these things are the ones I was going to buy from Juan Deer for *The Trading Post.*"

"Let's carry them to the bus," Ricky said eagerly. "They're really ours."

A noise from the outer room caused everyone to cease talking.

"What was that?" Pete whispered, going to the small exit to look.

As he peered out the boy was just in time to see a man dashing toward the ladder.

"Stop!" Pete shouted, crawling out the opening after the fleeing figure.

Mr. Hollister and Ricky followed. When the man reached the ladder, the light was strong enough for them to recognize him. Dredmon Gross!

"Hold on there!" Mr. Hollister cried.

But Mr. Gross had no intention of being caught by the Hollisters. He was up the ladder like a spider.

"We mustn't lose him!" Mr. Hollister cried.

Before they could grab the ladder, Mr. Gross began to pull it up. Pete, in the lead, stretched high, his fingertips catching the last rung. But he could not hold on. Quickly the ladder disappeared over the top of the cliff.

"He's gone!" Ricky shouted.

"And we're trapped down here!" Pete exclaimed.

CHAPTER 17

The Hidden Letter

THE TRICK Mr. Gross had played on the Hollisters stunned them. Without a ladder their escape from the cliff dwelling was cut off. For how long, none of them could guess.

"We'll have to find some way out!" Mr. Hollister said determinedly. "Perhaps if Pete stands on my shoulders and Ricky gets up on his, we may be able to reach the top of the opening."

"Okay, Dad. I think we can do it!" Pete responded hopefully.

He hopped onto his father's back and climbed to his sturdy shoulders.

"Okay, Ricky, hop up!"

But the smaller boy was nowhere in sight. He had run off through the empty rooms of the ancient cliff dwelling.

"Ricky! Come back here!" Mrs. Hollister shouted.

When he did not answer, Pam begged to take his place. But Mrs. Hollister said she did not think it was exactly safe for any of the children to climb out.

"Gross or Rattler may be waiting up there," she said. "They know now that their game is up and may try to harm us. Anyway, we should find Ricky."

165

A search began but when they did not find him, Mr. Hollister stepped out of one of the doorways to the terrace. At this moment a pebble fell down in front of his face and he looked up. There was Ricky, scaling the side of the cliff!

"Ricky! Be careful!" Mr. Hollister cried out.

The boy stopped climbing for a moment and called back, "I'm all right. There are lots of rocks to hold on to. I have to get that bad man!"

Once more he began making his way up the side of the cliff, grabbing out-jutting rocks and finding indentations for his feet.

"That son of ours is a dare-devil," Mr. Hollister told his wife as she too looked. "Well, if he can climb up there, so can I."

Ricky was scaling the side of the cliff!

"I can make it too, Dad," Pete said bravely.

His father thought this over a minute, then said, "Pete, I believe you'd better stay here with the rest of our family and help protect the treasure."

"All right, Dad."

Mr. Hollister stood directly under Ricky and watched hawklike in case he should have to catch him. But the boy was as sure-footed as a mountain goat and soon was at the top. He waved down to them.

"Okay! I made it, Dad!"

His father waved back. "Fine, son. Wait for me. I'm coming up."

Mr. Hollister removed his jacket and handed it to his wife. Getting a good hold in the face of the rocky cliff, he began to climb slowly.

"Be careful," Sue called up to him. "I don't want a busted Daddy."

This made Mr. Hollister laugh, so that for a second he lost his grip and began to slide backward. As his wife gasped, he grabbed a jutting rock and steadied himself. Then he began the perilous ascent again. Here and there he found toe holds made by the ancient Indians.

He could not climb as fast as Ricky had, but gradually Mr. Hollister pulled himself to the top and joined his son. He waited to catch his breath, then cupped his hands and shouted down:

"We'll be back as soon as we can!"

After he and Ricky had left, Mrs. Hollister suggested that she and the other children go into the treasure room and find out in what condition the stolen property was. Sue was so tired that her mother arranged a blanket for the drowsy child to lie on, and in no time the little girl was sound asleep.

While Pete put new candles in the holders, Pam and Holly sat down on the floor and tried to fit the turquoise stones back into the bracelets. When the girls had reset the stones as best they could, they started to sort a pile of Yumatan dolls and children's costumes which were piled up in a disorderly heap.

"Let's take these things out into the daylight where we can examine them better," Pam suggested.

Carrying one armful after another, the sisters lugged the articles through the inner room to the cave opening. In the bright sunlight all the things

"What's that?" Holly asked.

appeared to be in good condition in spite of the way they had been handled.

As the girls smoothed out the wrinkled things and put them in orderly stacks, Pam picked up a piece of paper which lay between a red shirt and a feathered headdress.

"What's that?" Holly asked.

"It looks like part of a letter," Pam replied, spreading the paper out flat with her fingers.

"The writing on it's pretty faded," Holly observed. "It must be old. Can you read it, Pam?"

At first her sister had trouble making out the scrawled letters, but presently she read slowly:

heard—this story—from a dying Indian Claims he was —the only survivor near the landslide. Watched until the dust settled. Made a map with new landmarks of the covered entrance to the turquoise mine. Hid the map under the turquoise of his silver bracelet. Had a leaf design. It was lost many years ago.

"That's why the bracelets were taken apart—to find the map!" Pam exclaimed. "I wonder where Mr. Gross got this letter."

"Let's tell Mother and Pete about it," Holly urged and the two girls dashed back.

Pam reread the letter and the others became very excited. But a moment later Pete said, worried:

"Do you think Mr. Gross found the map?"

"He probably did," Pam sighed. "And right in my bracelet or Holly's."

"Maybe not," her mother said encouragingly. "If

"It's full of jewelry!"

he had, I doubt that he would have come here."

"That's right," said Pete. "He would have been off hunting for the turquoise mine."

While Holly was listening, she idly lifted a small rug loom used by Indian children. Beneath it was an ornate box painted in bright colors.

"This looks like a jewel box," she thought.

The little girl had some trouble opening the tight latch, but when the top flew up she gasped in surprise.

"It's full of jewelry!" she exclaimed, lifting out a handful of turquoise pins and earrings.

"And there are two bracelets at the bottom!" Pam cried, looking inside.

She picked them up. One had a leaf design worked into the silver and held a beautiful turquoise stone.

"Maybe this is the secret bracelet," Holly said. "Let me look under the stone."

Pam handed it to her and she tried to pry the turquoise up with her fingernail.

"Oh, it's in tight," she said. "Pete, will you lend me your knife, please?"

"Sure."

Pete flipped open the blade and handed the knife to her.

"Be careful!" her mother warned. "Don't break it!"

Holly gingerly dug around the edge of the stone for a few moments when *flip* the turquoise popped out. The gasp that Holly gave woke Sue up. "Look!" Holly exclaimed. "There's a tiny paper in here!"

The others looked on astounded as the little girl opened a tiny yellowed sheet.

"What funny markings!" Pete said. "Maybe it's a map to the lost turquoise mine!"

Holly asked her mother gleefully what she thought.

"It could be," Mrs. Hollister replied enthusiastically. "If this mark is Pilar Punta, then the arrow from it leads past the two X's which could be the twin caves."

"And the next arrow points to that circle," Pam added. "Oh, I'm sure it's the lost mine!"

"I hope Daddy hurries back so we can get out of here and start hunting," said Holly eagerly.

"But if the Indians don't know where Pilar Punta is, how can we find it?" Pete asked as he put the map into his pocket.

"We'll keep trying, anyhow," Pam said with de-

They raced along the terrace to the tower.

termination. "Mother, wasn't the landslide some-where on the opposite side of this canyon?"

"Yes, dear, in that general direction."

"Then maybe if we could get a good look at the places over there from real high up, we might see Pilar Punta."

"You mean from a plane?" Pete asked.

"No. I mean from the tower. Let's see if we can get into it."

She started off, with Pete and Holly close on her heels. They raced along the terrace until they came to the tower.

"There ought to be an entrance some place," Pete mused.

If so, it had long ago been blocked off. But each

of the children began pulling at the earth and stones. Suddenly one came loose. Then several tumbled down.

Through the opening they could see a spiraling stone stairway built into the wall all the way to the top. The children scrambled up it and peered out two openings which overlooked the canyon.

"This must have been the old look-out," Pete remarked. "I suppose an Indian was stationed here at all times to watch for approaching enemies."

"How high we are!" Holly exclaimed, looking across to the opposite side of the canyon with its lovely rainbow coloring. A white cloud hugged the mountain top. "Look! What's that sticking up into the cloud?" the girl asked.

"What's that sticking up into the cloud?"

Pam glued her eyes to the distant object. "It's a peak of some kind," she said, studying a small spire that pointed like a giant needle against the white fluff.

"Do you suppose that's Pilar Punta?" Holly asked.

The idea sent a chill of excitement racing down the spines of the three children.

"It does look like a pillar!" Pete shouted. "Oh, Holly, if you've discovered it, then with the map we can solve the mystery."

He and the girls climbed down the steps and hurried to report what they had seen. Mrs. Hollister smiled and Sue clapped her hands gleefully.

"When Ricky and Daddy get back," she said, "we can drive out and find the turquoise mountain!"

As the minutes ticked by, they wondered what was keeping the others.

"They've been gone more than two hours," Mrs. Hollister said, a frown of worry crossing her face.

After another twenty minutes all of them became alarmed.

"Mother, do you suppose—" Pam began, then stopped. But to herself she said anxiously, "Oh, I hope no harm has come to Dad and Ricky."

CHAPTER 18

A Treasure Hunt

SUDDENLY a voice boomed down over the edge of the cliff.

"We're back! Where's everybody?"

"John!" Mrs. Hollister cried out. "Are you all right? Is Ricky with you?"

"Yes, and I have a ladder," he called.

In a moment a light metal ladder appeared down the wedge-shaped cut in the rock. First Ricky, then Mr. Hollister hurried down it.

"We have wonderful news," the boy said breathlessly. "Officer Martinez captured Mr. Gross and Rattler too."

"Crickets!" Pete exclaimed.

"The men confessed," Ricky added importantly. "They stole the things from Juan Deer and Rattler hid the rug near the pueblo so the Yumatans would be blamed. And Mr. Gross stole Holly's bracelet."

"We have wonderful news too," Pam announced. "All the missing things are here!"

As her father exclaimed in amazement, another voice called down from the rim of the crevice. "I'm ready to help you, Mr. Hollister!"

"All right, Swift Eagle. But you'd better come down here first."

When the Indian reached the bottom of the ladder, he heard the announcement and congratulated the children for finding the missing articles. Then Holly grabbed his hand and said:

"We found the map to your lost turquoise mine!"

The governor was so astonished he was speechless but Mr. Hollister asked, "You found it? Where?"

Holly told them while Pete showed the letter and the map.

"This is amazing!" Swift Eagle exclaimed.

Pete related how Holly had spotted a pinnacle in the distance which they thought might be Pilar Punta and the Indian went to look at it.

"We'll go there tomorrow," Swift Eagle promised. "I believe you have solved the mystery about the mine. And now I'll help you carry the stolen articles to the bus."

What a job it was, toting the loads up the ladder and over the rough ground! But finally everything was packed into the bus. It was so full there was little room left for passengers.

"I guess," Swift Eagle laughed, "that several Hollisters will have to ride with me!"

The children rode with the Indian and both drivers went directly to State Police Headquarters. To their surprise Juan Deer was there talking to Patrolman Martinez.

"All your stolen goods have been recovered," Mr.

"What a job it was!"

Hollister told the old Indian. "They're in our bus."

Tears came to Juan Deer's eyes when he stepped outside and saw the contents of *The Chaparral.*

"I'd still like to buy them," said Mr. Hollister.

"Thank you," Juan Deer replied. "I like to give them to Hollisters but Juan Deer not have much money."

After he and Mr. Hollister had arranged for the purchase and shipping of the articles, Pete told him about the letter and map and the trip planned for the next morning.

"Juan Deer hope story true," the old Indian smiled.

The children rose early the following day to prepare for the expedition. After breakfast Swift Eagle and Officer Martinez arrived. The policeman said Rattler had admitted taking the note from a dying cowboy, who had heard the story of the buried mine from an Indian. He had foolishly told Gross about it instead of Swift Eagle.

"Let's start our 'venture," Sue spoke up impatiently.

Everyone climbed into the bus and Mr. Hollister said, "Swift Eagle, will you be our navigator to Pilar Punta?"

He drove down the highway a short distance, then the Indian governor told him to turn left into an overgrown side road. It wound up and down through little arroyos and sand hills.

After Mr. Hollister had driven several miles, Swift Eagle told him to park. From there the treasure hunters stumbled, crawled and climbed among the cedars and chimesa bushes. As they came to the end of a gorge, Pam exclaimed:

"There it is, Dad! I see Pilar Punta!"

The pinnacle rose just ahead of them, looming majestically in the morning sun.

"It's well hidden," said Swift Eagle. "The Yumatans never come out this way. That's why the pillar was not known."

When they reached the base of it, Pete consulted the secret map, guiding the others in the direction the arrow indicated.

"The old landslide covered this place well," Officer Martinez remarked. "If we had come much later, I'm afraid that Nature would have hidden her secret from us forever."

Half a mile beyond, in a gorge, Ricky and his brother cried out together, "A cave!"

To the left, partly obscured by piñon and juniper bushes was a tiny opening in the mountainside. The policeman flashed a light inside and reported the cave was small and bare.

Looking at the map, Pete traced a line directly opposite the cave and started walking. In a few moments he shouted to the others, "Here's the second cave!"

They ran up excitedly. The opening was no larger than an Indian drum.

"The clues are working!" Pam said excitedly. "Next we'll find the mine!"

Again Pete consulted the map and led them to

"It should be right here."

the base of a steep cliff, at the bottom of which rested several huge boulders.

"According to the map, it should be right here," the boy stated. "Everybody give me a hand with these boulders."

The men and boys pushed against the huge stones with all their strength. Finally the rocks yielded and rolled away, revealing a small opening.

The policeman tried to look in with his light but could see nothing.

"Ricky," said Mr. Hollister, "that hole's hardly big enough for you to squeeze through, but do you want to try it?"

"You bet!"

The boy, taking the flashlight, wriggled inside until his feet had entirely disappeared. "Hey," he called back, "there's a big room in here and some tools." He handed out a crude stone axe. "And little blue lines on the walls."

"You've found our turquoise mine!" Swift Eagle exclaimed joyfully. "Now we will no longer be poor!"

Working feverishly with the axe, stones and their bare hands, the Indian treasure hunters enlarged the hole enough so they could all enter and gaze at the veins of turquoise. Then with Swift Eagle and the children humming happily, they walked back through the gorge and rode to Agua Verde.

"I don't know what to say to you Happy Hollister children," Swift Eagle smiled, when they reached the hotel, "except to wish that you were Yumatans."

"I'd like that," said Holly. "Then we could be cousins to Red Feather and Blue Feather."

That afternoon Indians with modern picks and shovels set out to start working the mine at once. Word came to the Hollisters that Indy Roades and War Horse would always receive part of the profits because of their help in solving the mystery.

"Goody!" said Sue. "Everything's turning out happy."

The next morning every Indian in Agua Verde smiled broadly at the Hollisters as they passed by.

"I think they're up to something," Mr. Hollister said to his wife. "I can tell by their faces."

About noontime a delegation of Indians led by Juan Deer came to see the Hollisters at the hotel.

"Yumatans invite you to pueblo supper tonight," the old man said.

"Thank you," Mrs. Hollister replied. "We shall be happy to accept."

Toward the end of the day the streets of Agua Verde were deserted. All the Indians and many of the other townspeople had gone to the pueblo. When the Hollisters arrived, the place was buzzing with activity. The children and their parents were ushered to the dwelling of Swift Eagle. Smilingly he presented each one with a colorful ceremonial blanket, and feathers for their hair.

"Please honor us by wearing them now," he requested.

At first the Hollisters were a little embarrassed,

"I pronounce you all members of the tribe!"

but they put on their gifts. Then, as the drums began
to beat, the visitors were led to an Indian feast in
the center of the plaza where a huge fire was blazing.
Over it a whole lamb, suspended on stout sticks, was
roasting.

After everyone had been served large portions
of this and other good things to eat, there were
dances and chanting for the Hollisters' entertainment. Finally Swift Eagle, wearing pink trousers and
a purple velvet shirt, solemnly arose. Wampum hung
from his neck, and around his waist was a silver
concho belt. He looked directly at the Hollisters and
said:

"My people have gathered tonight to perform a
very unusual ceremony. Po-da, will you step forward?
And Red Feather and Blue Feather?"

The lieutenant-governor walked with dignified steps to Swift Eagle's side, a wooden bowl in his hands. The Indian children followed.

"Now we are ready to make our good white friends members of the Yumatan tribe," Swift Eagle announced solemnly. "Will the Hollisters join us?"

Amazed and bursting with pride, the visitors from Shoreham walked slowly to where the governor and the others stood. Swift Eagle raised his right hand and a low chanting began in the crowd.

Po-da moved in front of the governor, extending the bowl to him. The Hollisters could see that it contained fine white corn meal. Swift Eagle took a small portion in his fingers and put the grains in his mouth.

His lieutenant next offered the corn to Red Feather and Blue Feather, who did exactly as their grandfather had. Po-da was next. Then he passed the bowl to each of the Hollisters. They too ate a few grains of the corn.

"Now I pronounce the Happy Hollisters members of the Yumatan tribe!" Swift Eagle proclaimed. "May this pueblo be one of your homes as long as you live. And we hope you will come here often."

The drums throbbed and the chanting continued.

"*Hiyo, hiyo, hiyo witsn nayo*" was repeated over and over.

The new Anglo members of the tribe were so impressed they could not say much. But they did shake hands with Swift Eagle and Po-da and thank them.

Then Pam, Holly and Sue hugged Blue Feather and Pete slapped Red Feather on the shoulder.

"Now we're your really true cousins!" Holly said.

"Come, we will do a friendship dance," Red Feather said, leading the Hollister children to where an Indian boy sat on the ground beating a drum. "Take off your blankets if you wish."

"The new Yumatans will dance alone in a circle for a few minutes," Blue Feather said after the children had handed the gifts to their parents. "Then we Indians will join you."

Pam immediately started to dance, and Pete took up the rhythm behind her. Next came little Sue, followed by Ricky and Holly.

As the Hollisters circled, Blanca fluttered overhead and landed on Holly's left wrist. This gesture of friendship was the sign for the Yumatan children to join the dance. They fell in line with the Hollisters as the grownups began to chant a merry tune.

"Finding an Indian treasure is the most fun ever," Holly giggled as she and her brothers and sisters danced round and round with their Indian cousins.